A Land
Remembered

Volume Two

To Grace,
with best wishes,

John Smith

3-8-03

a novel by

Patrick D. Smith

A Land Remembered

Volume Two
Student Edition

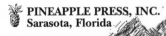 **PINEAPPLE PRESS, INC.**
Sarasota, Florida

Inquiries should be addressed to:
Pineapple Press, Inc.
P.O. Box 3889
Sarasota, Florida 34230

www.pineapplepress.com

LIBRARY OF CONGRESS CATALOGING IN PUBLICATION DATA

Smith, Patrick D., 1927–
  A land remembered.– Student ed., 1st ed.
    p.   cm.
  Summary: Traces the story of the MacIvey family of Florida from 1858 to 1968.
        Volume 1 : ISBN 1-56164-223-1 (pb : alk. paper) ISBN 1-56164-230-4
        (hb : alk. paper)
        Volume 2 : ISBN 1-56164-224-X (pb : alk. paper) ISBN 1-56164-231-2
        (hb : alk. paper)
  [1. Family life–Florida–Fiction. 2. Florida–Fiction.] I. Title.

PZ7.S65748 Lan 2001
[Fic]–dc21

                                                                00-053749

First Edition
10 9 8 7 6 5 4 3 2 1

Design by Carol Tornatore Creative Design
Printed in the United States of America

To the grandchildren —

Dan, Kimberly, Joshua, Matthew, and Alex

with love from "Grampy"

and

To Grace

Please remember me,

Grandmother and Granddaddy

Acknowledgments

This student edition was the idea of Mary Lee Powell and Tillie Newhart, who labored on the preparation of the text. They, like many other Florida teachers, often read this favorite Florida historical novel to their classes, abridging as they read to a level appropriate for younger students. Now, with the help of a Martha Robertson Harris Scholarship through Delta Kappa Gamma Society International, they have made it available to all teachers and students in this abridged edition in two volumes.

Mary Lee Powell recently retired after teaching for thirty years in Osceola County, Florida. She has won numerous awards, including Osceola District Teacher of the Year and Disney's Teacher Merit Award. Tillie Newhart has taught for ten years in Osceola County. She was recently named Elementary Social Studies Teacher of the Year for the Osceola School District. Together they initiated a community-wide effort to involve students in developing a museum of Florida history. The Cannery Museum, located at 901 Virginia Avenue, St. Cloud, Florida, is recognized nationally as the only student-run museum in the country. The students' exhibits display many of the scenes of Florida history they learned about in *A Land Remembered*.

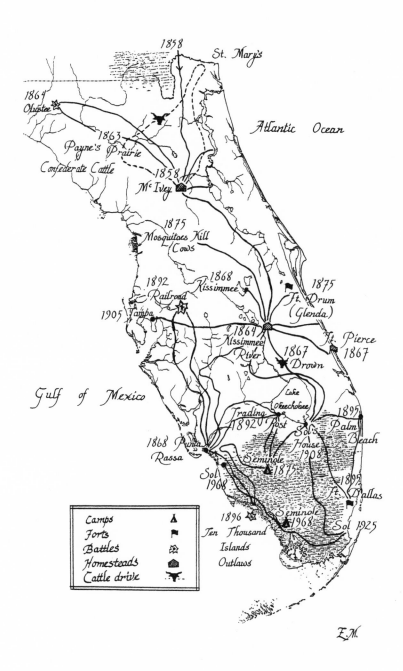

1858

St. Mary's

1864
Olustee

Atlantic Ocean

1863
Payne's Prairie
Confederate Cattle

1858
Mc Ivey

1875
Mosquitoes Kill
Cows

1892
Railroad

1868
Kissimmee

1875
Ft. Drum
(Glenda)

1905 Tampa

1864
Kissimmee
River

1867
Drown

Ft. Pierce
1867

Gulf of Mexico

Lake
Okeechobee

Trading
1892 Post

1895
Palm
Beach

Sol's
House
1908

1868 Punta
Rassa

Seminole
1875

Sol
1968

1892
Ft. Dallas

Seminole
1968

Sol 1925

1896
Ten Thousand
Islands
Outlaws

Camps
Forts
Battles
Homesteads
Cattle drive

E.M.

🐃

"Oh, no!" Zech said, looking down at the cow with its stomach slit open. "That's the fourth one in two days."

Skillit dismounted and examined the carcass. "All they took again was the heart and liver. They must have a powerful cravin' for that kind of meat. It sho' is a waste."

"I sure would like to get my sights on whoever's doing this," Zech said.

Skillit remounted and said, "They keep this up we won't have much to brand."

"Or sell either. Let's take what we got on back to the corral."

Zech and Skillit popped their whips, causing the cows to lurch forward. Far in the distance smoke drifted upward as Frog heated the branding iron, waiting.

It was late May, a month later than they usually completed the roundup, but his father, Tobias, had been sick again and insisted they wait until he could help. No amount of persuasion by Emma or Zech could keep him at the house, and Zech worried constantly as he watched his father become more gaunt from the hot sun and the hard work of branding.

Frog opened the gate at the sound of approaching hooves, then slammed it shut when the cows rushed inside. Tobias said to him, "How many did you count?"

"Nineteen."

"That's what I got too. I thought there would be more than that."

Zech reined his horse and said, "They done it some more, Pappa. All shot in the head and the bellies slit open. That makes about forty so far."

"How long you figure they been dead when you found the last ones?" Tobias asked.

"Not long. No more than a day, maybe less."

"Them thieves is getting awful brave. They must be out there sommers right now, watching us. This keeps up we might all have to go hunting, but this time it won't be for four-legged varmints. I can't understand why any man would shoot a cow for the heart and liver. He could get as much meat out of a rabbit."

"Just pure meanness," Skillit said. "Maybe they move on soon and let us be. They don't, we ought to set their behinds on fire with the Winchesters."

"You want us to go looking for them?" Zech asked. "Me and Skillit and Frog could ride the woods at night. They bound to build a fire, 'less they eat raw meat, and that ain't likely."

"No, better not," Tobias responded. "I got a notion that sooner or later they'll come to us. And besides that, we got to get ready for the grazing drive. We're late already."

"If it suits all of you," Frog said, "let's quit the jawin' and get done with the branding. I don't like to be late for supper since Miz Glenda started making them huckleberry pies."

"She's spoiled us all, pure and simple," Tobias said. "First thing you know we'll be taking baths before having vittles."

"That wouldn't be no bad idea for Frog," Skillit said. "If he'd wash up some every month or so them buzzards wouldn't follow us all the time like they do. Pearlie Mae asked me just the other day if we had skunks in the barn, and it was Frog feedin' his horse."

"Ain't nothing in the world stinks worse than your sweat," Frog said. "It was you she smelled, not me."

"No wonder Glenda thinks everbody out here is crazy," Zech said. "Let's go on and get done with the work. I got a chore to do at the house."

"I know you have a lot of chores," Frog said. "That new wife, Glenda, keeps you very busy. I knowed a man once who got hitched and his wife had him doin' so much work, the first you know he got so skinny a dog buried him, thinkin' he was a bone."

Skillit suddenly grabbed Frog, lifted him off the ground and pointed his backside upward. He said, "Get the brandin' iron, Mistuh Zech! See can you pick it up! Then stick it to him and we'll see how loud a frog can holler!"

Zech took the glowing iron from the fire and held it three inches from Frog's rear, singeing his pants. Frog shouted, "I was just kiddin', Mister Zech! Don't put that thing to me!"

"He bellers loud, don't he?" Skillit chuckled, releasing his grip. "He'll draw all the 'gators outen the swamp fo' a chomp of frog meat."

Frog stood up and rubbed his pants as Tobias said, "Lordy, Lordy, I hope them rustlers ain't watching us now. If they are, they'll think this outfit is run by a bunch of loons. No wonder they ain't scared of us."

"Don't you worry none about that, Mistuh Tobias," Skillit said. "We jus funnin' now. We come on them polecats, the funnin' stops. Ain't gone be no play time with them."

"That's right," Frog agreed. "It's gone be a whole lot worse than a brandin' iron and singed britches."

"I still think we ought to go after them," Zech said. "If we don't find them first, they'll do us just like somebody did the dogs."

Glenda became a member of the MacIvey clan with ease, and Emma liked her immensley, finding in her the companionship of a daughter she always wanted. Glenda refused to stand idly by as Emma and Pearlie Mae prepared meals. She peeled potatoes and chopped onions, reddening her eyes, and when there was nothing more to do she went alone into the woods and gathered berries for pies. In her spare moments she changed the bare cabin Zech built for them into a home, putting up curtains and covering the bedroom floor with a braided rug, decorating the walls with little knickknacks she brought from

Fort Drum. Zech enjoyed her pampering more than he would admit, and each evening as he headed for the hammock he ran Ishmael faster than usual.

She also convinced him to spend one hour each night beside a coal oil lamp, learning to read and write. At first he resisted, but as the words gradually took on meaning he went at it eagerly, realizing a previously unknown world was opening for him.

Emma watched it all with deep satisfaction, knowing that when children came Glenda could give them something more than she had been able to offer Zech, a chance to break free and do something more than grub for survival. There were other things in the world besides planting collards and skinning coons and herding cows and fighting wolves, things such as books and music and church services, and Glenda would lead the way. These things were now beyond Tobias, and maybe Zech too, but her grandchildren could sample them if they so desired. At least they would have the opportunity to choose.

It was not that Emma regretted any part of her own life. If the choice were offered to her again, she would follow Tobias into the wilderness with only a frying pan and the clothes on her back. She never looked back or complained about things she might have missed along the way. She wanted a better life for Zech and his wife and for those yet to come. If someday she could be surrounded by grandchildren whose faces were filled with joy and play, and not just work, then the long and difficult journey would have been worthwhile.

Emma took the coffee pot from the stove, poured two cups and put them on the table. She said to Glenda, "Come and sit with me. Those men will be coming in soon with their stomachs growling. We can have a few minutes of peace and rest before they get here."

Glenda sipped the coffee, and then she said, "I don't see how you cooked for so many before you had Pearlie Mae to help. It must have been a chore."

"Oh, it wasn't so bad. It's as easy to cook for six as it is for

4

three. You just add a little extra to the pot. And there were times when the only things I had to cook were cattail flour and coon meat. That makes it simple. You should have seen poor old Skillit when he came to us. He was so hungry he would have eaten boiled cypress bark. Frog and Bonzo were just about as bad off too."

"We knew hard times too, but not that bad," Glenda said. "When we first came to Fort Drum it was nothing but wilderness. Daddy brought the lumber down from Jacksonville in an ox cart and built the store himself. It was a long time after that when the little settlement began to grow up around the store. I can remember Daddy going to Fort Capron to meet the schooner and bringing back goods a piece at a time, whatever he could get. Sometimes he traded a few turns of cloth for deer meat, and a sack of nails for potatoes. Zech doesn't know this about my family and I haven't told him. He thinks the store has always been there, stocked with food and other things. But it hasn't."

Emma put down her cup and took Glenda's hand in hers. "Glenda, I know why you're helping me so much in the kitchen, even doing the wash when Pearlie Mae could do it. Just don't try so hard. You don't have to prove anything to Zech. If you asked him how I spend each day, he couldn't tell you. He knows I always have food ready when he's hungry, and I wash his clothes, but that's all. He's not here during the lonely times. What he needs now is a wife to love, not a cook and housekeeper. He's had that all his life, and that's all he's ever had."

"I'm not sure love is enough by itself," Glenda said. "I know it has taken hard work as well as love for you to do the things you've done to keep your men alive. When we first met, Zech thought I wouldn't be up to it, that all I wanted was to be in Jacksonville and go to theaters and dances. I've never wanted such things, and I can't even imagine myself married to some bank clerk in Jacksonville who plays the piano. I want to be here, riding with Zech, being his partner as well as his wife, chasing cows if he wants me to, doing whatever he wants and being whatever he wants me to be. I love him that much."

"Zech will make you a kind and loving man, like Tobias, in his own way," Emma said. "But there's one thing you'll have to remember. He was brought up in the wilderness, and that's all he's ever known. It's inside him. He didn't shy away from you because he thought you couldn't live out here. It was because he thought he wasn't good enough for you, and that if he married you, you would make him leave the wilderness and go elsewhere. This he will never do. You'll have to understand that, Glenda, and be patient with him. Zech will do the best he can to make you happy. He may not always show it, like his father sometimes doesn't show it, but he will."

"You know," Glenda said, "I'm glad you're you, Emma. I could never talk like this with my mother."

"You'll never know how many times I've yearned to just sit and talk with another woman, like we're doing now. That's what I've missed the most. I'm so glad you're here, and I'm proud to have you as my daughter. "

"While we're talking woman talk, I have a secret to share," Glenda said, smiling. "I'm going to have a baby!"

"Oh, Glenda, that's wonderful!" Emma exclaimed. "I'm so happy for you and Zech! Have you told Zech? He hasn't mentioned it."

"No. I'm not going to for a while yet. And I don't want you to either."

"Glenda, I don't understand," Emma said, puzzled. "Why would you keep it from him? He'll know sooner or later."

"I want to go on the drive with all of you. If Zech knew about this he wouldn't let me go. I just know he wouldn't."

"The drive isn't as important as this," Emma reasoned. "I have to go because I'm the cook, but Pearlie Mae can stay here and look after you. You shouldn't hide this from Zech."

"Going with Zech this time is important to me. I've got to prove to him I can do it. I know it would be foolish to take the baby out

6

there next summer, and that's why I must go now. I just have to, Emma!"

"I've already told you. You don't have to prove anything to Zech! If you'll stay, I'll stay with you. The men go on roundups by themselves and take along smoked beef and hardtack. They can do the same thing on a drive. It would be hard for Pearlie Mae to go by herself and look after her boys and cook too. And besides that, Zech and Tobias know how to cook rabbits and coons. They'll do fine without us."

"No, I want to go," Glenda insisted. "I won't stay behind!"

"Is it really that important to you?"

"Yes, it is."

"Well, I'll say one thing," Emma said, "you're a MacIvey for sure. You're as stubborn as Tobias or Zech ever hoped to be. I'll share your secret under one condition."

"What's that?" Glenda asked, glad that Emma was about to agree.

"If you get to feeling poorly you and I will turn back. This baby means more to me than all the gold in Punta Rassa, and I know it would to Zech too. Will you promise me this?"

"Yes, I promise. But I know I'll be fine."

"When we get back this time we'll really have something to celebrate," Emma said. "We'll have a party, the first one we've ever had out here. You can make the pies, and I'll do the rest, and we'll invite your mother and father."

"That would be wonderful," Glenda said. "And when the baby comes, we'll have another. It should be close to Christmas. We'll have our own Christmas frolic."

"I don't know how I'll be able to keep this to myself, but I'll try. And I'm so happy, Glenda. I've wanted a baby around this place for such a long time. I just might take it away from you."

"We'll share," Glenda laughed. "And if it's twins, you can have one and I'll take the other."

CHAPTER TWENTY-FIVE

One thousand and eighty sets of six-foot horns bobbed in unison as the herd was prodded from the main corral and turned to the northwest. The men were on horseback to the rear and on the sides, followed by Emma and Glenda in the buckboard and Pearlie Mae with her load of jumping jack boys in the ox wagon.

By noon of the first day Glenda's skin was burned tomato red by the prairie sun, and she retreated from the open buckboard to the protection of the covered wagon. Emma greased her neck, face and arms with lard to ease the stinging pain, and she did not complain. The next morning she was back on the buckboard wearing long sleeves, a bandanna around her neck and a sunbonnet.

Emma watched Glenda constantly, begging her not to carry buckets heavy with water from nearby springs when they made camp, Glenda doing it anyway. No one seemed to notice this extra attention Emma was giving Glenda as she insisted on doing her share of camp chores.

One morning Zech awoke to find Glenda sitting upright, frozen with terror, her eyes transfixed on a rattlesnake coiled at her feet. He whispered, "Don't move. It just came in to get warm. I've found them in my boots and in the bedroll with me. If you stay still it won't strike."

She watched horrified as Zech reached slowly for the rifle, aimed it and blew the snake's head ten feet from the tent, its headless body then thrashing violently as blood gushed onto the blanket.

She screamed, "Get that thing out of here! Get it out!"

He said calmly, "It can't hurt you now. I'll skin it out for breakfast."

"You'll what?"

"That's good eating, Glenda. Tastes like chicken. We have it all the time on drives when we get tired of beef."

Glenda was about to gag when Emma rushed into the tent, alarmed by the gunshot and screaming. "What is it?" she asked anxiously. "Are you all right, Glenda?"

"Snake," Zech said, pointing. "I'll have it ready time you get the frying pan hot."

"Oh. You sure you're all right, Glenda?"

"I'm fine. It just scared me, that's all."

"I won't tell you what happened first time one of those varmints crawled in bed with me," Emma said. "It'd ruin your breakfast."

Glenda dressed shakily, came outside and was greeted by the smell of meat sizzling in the cast-iron skillet. She sat by Zech as he put a chunk of fried snake onto a tin plate and started eating. The cooked flesh was white, like chicken breast, and she accepted the bite he handed her. She put it in her mouth, chewed and swallowed; then she said, "Not bad. It does taste something like chicken. I know you like it, so you can have the rest of it. I'll just have coffee and a biscuit. "

Zech gulped down the chunk and took another piece from the frying pan. He said, "Just wait till you try some of Mamma's fried rabbit brains for breakfast. It's even better than snake."

"Not now, Zech," Glenda said, nibbling the biscuit. "Tell me about it later. I've got to go to the tent for a minute. I forgot something."

He kept munching as she went around the side of the tent and then ran for the nearest palmetto clump to throw up.

They drifted lazily, finding abundant grass and remaining until it was cropped short, spending days under clear blue skies not torn asunder by violent thunderstorms, enjoying gentle, cooling rains in late afternoon. Glenda enjoyed the brilliant rainbows forming glowing arches over the flat prairie land. This was her first trip inland, and she was fascinated by seemingly endless flights of herons and egrets and ibises, and by herds of deer galloping close by, stopping momentarily to stare at them curiously, then bounding away.

One night the cry of wolves sounded through the stillness, causing the cattle to low nervously. Glenda stayed up all night, watching wide-eyed as glowing fires pushed back the darkness, the men like roaming shadows as they circled the herd. She did not fully understand the danger involved and was unaware of how quickly disaster could strike, but the sight and sound of it thrilled her because this was what she wanted to be a part of. Here things were happening, things beyond human control; and there was no house to go into for protection, no doors to lock or windows to close. It was them against nature, winner take all; it frightened her. She was beginning to respect Tobias and Emma and Zech even more for having survived a lifetime of this, facing it again and again without fear, then coming back for more.

When they reached the edge of the salt marsh, they were met by four armed riders who charged the lead steer, turning the herd away, toward the river. Tobias and Zech rode forward as Frog and Skillit popped their whips, regaining control of the herd and holding them in a circle.

Tobias noticed cows scattered across the marsh as he rode to the line of men. He stopped directly in front of them and said, "What do you mean turning my herd like that? You could 'a caused a stampede!"

One man moved his horse forward and said, "You can't come in here. You'll have to go sommers else."

"How come?" Tobias asked. "We been here ever time we wanted to and nobody stopped us. Who says we can't come in now?"

"This says," the man answered, waving a rifle. "We got here first. 'Less you want to risk getting shot, you'll move on away from here. I got six more men down there, all armed."

"You ain't got the right!" Tobias said angrily. "This place belongs to us as much as it does to you, and my cows needs the salt. We're coming in!"

Four levers pumped as four Winchesters were pointed at Tobias and Zech. Tobias looked at the barrels and said, "This ain't going to do nobody any good. I got more riders and guns too. There's grass enough for everbody."

"I say there ain't. The first cow you move in here gets shot, and ever one that follows gets shot, and ever drover too. You just better back off, mister, and think about it."

Tobias wheeled the horse without further comment and rode back to the buckboard, popping his whip two times as a signal for Frog and Skillit to come in. Emma immediately noticed his stern expression and said, "What's happening, Tobias? Who are those men?"

"They're trying to turn us away."

"We got as much right to be here as anybody, Pappa," Zech said. "We ought to start us a war."

"You don't know what a war is," Tobias responded. "If I have to I will, but it ain't a pleasant thing to see. We'll talk first."

As soon as Frog and Skillit rode in, Tobias said, "Only way we're going to get in down there is to shoot our way in. What does everybody say we do?"

"How many men they got?" Frog asked.

"There's four over there, and they claim to have six more."

"Well, they's four of us," Frog said, "and if the women shoot from up here, that cuts down the odds some. I say we have at it."

"What about you, Skillit?"

"I don't know, Mistuh Tobias. Me, I don't mind goin' after them, but I sho' don't want Pearlie Mae an' the boys gettin' shot up. How come jus' us men can't do it?"

"We can. We'll leave the women out of it. First thing we'll do is stampede the herd right at them. Then we'll come in behind the cows and shoot everthing we see on a horse."

"No, Tobias!" Emma exclaimed loudly. "This has gone far enough! It's not worth it! We can go somewhere else!"

"If we back down now, Emma, it will happen again and again. Someday the range is going to get crowded. We just been lucky so far. We're going to have to fight for what belongs to us."

"Belongs to us?" Emma questioned. "We don't own this marsh, Tobias. If you got here first would you do the same thing those men are doing?"

Tobias didn't know exactly how to answer, never having faced such a situation. "Well, I don't know. But at least we ought to share."

"I'm not saying we shouldn't," Emma said. "But those men don't want to, and all the cows in the world aren't worth one of us getting killed. If somebody has to die for that grass down there, Tobias, which one of us do you say it is? Which one? Is it me, or Zech, or Skillit? Who? If you have the right to choose, which one of us do you want to see killed?"

"Aw, Emma, I don't want nobody killed," Tobias said meekly. "You know that. I don't have the right to say somebody has to die, and I wouldn't say it even if I did have the right."

"That's right, Tobias! You don't have the right! So stop this foolishness and move the herd across the river and away from here. I don't want to hear any more of it unless you say I'm the first to die. Do you hear me, Tobias?"

"Yes, Emma. I hear. And I'm sorry to have riled you up so. Sometimes us men are like frogs, we jump before we think and land right in a 'gator's mouth." Then he turned to the men and said, "What you staring at? You heard Emma! Get them cows moving toward the river!"

Frog said, "If that's what you want, Mister MacIvey. But I hope it comes a pure flood and they gets et up by skeeters."

Emma breathed a sign of relief as the men rode away. She said to Glenda, "That was close. And I couldn't have blamed them too much if they had charged in. There's grass enough to share, but some folks just don't want it that way."

"I'm learning," Glenda said. "I couldn't have pulled that off like you did no matter what. I would probably have pleaded with them. But I'm learning."

"You best. Things like this are going to happen more and more as time passes. It frightens me to think of it. If the men had been here alone, somebody would be dead by now. Maybe all of them."

Zech and Skillit rode ahead, buying cows and bringing them into the herd, and when they reached the Caloosahatchie River the total was just over two thousand.

Tobias wasn't interested as the sacks of gold coins were placed on the table. Zech took them out to the buckboard alone and gave Frog and Skillit their share. He told his mother and Glenda to take what they needed to buy supplies for the return trip and for whatever else they wanted.

When the two women came from the store both were dressed in jeans, denim shirts and boots, and Glenda had on a black felt hat. Her hair was tied in a ponytail that hung down her back.

Frog was the first to notice, and he said loudly, "Whoo-ee! Just look at that! Miz Emma and Miz Glenda got on britches!"

Glenda turned around and around, showing herself, and Zech said, "What's all this? You two look like drovers."

"It's silly for us to wear dresses on a drive," Glenda said. "This is much better. And Emma agrees. We've got as much right to wear britches as any of you."

"You have for a fact," Frog said, giggling. "And I think I'll just

13

go on in there and buy myself a dress. What color you think would look best on me, Zech?"

"Red. And you ought to get yourself some pink bloomers too. I'll help you put 'em on."

"Next one who makes a crack like that has dipped his last time in the cooking pot!" Emma snapped.

"I think you look just fine, Miz Emma," Frog said quickly. "You ought to have bought them things a long time ago. Now you an Miz Glenda can ride a hoss without sittin' sidesaddle."

Emma turned to Pearlie Mae. "You want some britches too?"

"No, ma'am, I better not," she responded, glancing at Skillit. "It take a pair big enough to stretch over a ox for me, more like a tent. I better not, Missus Emma."

Zech said, "If you don't mind, all of you go on back to the camp in the buckboard and leave me the wagon. I got something to haul. You can take Ishmael, Glenda."

"I'd like that," Glenda beamed. "It'll give me a chance to ride in my new outfit."

Emma frowned as Glenda mounted the horse, but she said nothing. The red ponytail swished from side to side as she tested Ishmael down the street and back. Then she trotted the horse ahead of the buckboard.

Zech went into the store and bought tools; then he drove the wagon to a lumberyard on the north edge of town. When he arrived back at the camp the wagon was stacked to capacity with lumber, its wheels groaning, and a load of cypress shingles was ordered for delivery the next morning.

Tobias stared as the oxen struggled in, puffing, and then he said, "What in thunder is all that for? You aim to pull that load slam across the prairie?"

"No, Pappa," Zech answered, climbing down. "It's for here. I'm going to build a cabin. If everbody pitches in and helps, we can do it in a couple of days."

"How come you want a cabin in Punta Rassa?"

14

"Just some place to stay when we come over here. And it would let folks know we own the land."

"I don't think nobody cares," Tobias said. "But we'll do it if that's what you want. It don't make no difference if we start back a couple of days later. Just so I get back pretty soon to see about my oranges."

Hammers pounded and saws pinged as the task took on the festive air of a barn raising. The women abandoned the cooking pot and supervised, telling the men to extend a wall here, put the stoop there, windows here and the door over yonder. By late afternoon the floor was down and all the framing up, and they went back into the town and ate the café completely out of fried chicken and fish.

Glenda enjoyed all of it, thrilled to be a part of people doing things, already planning in her mind where the bed should go, the color of curtains, a rug here and a shelf there.

That night after they had gone to bed Glenda still reeled with excitement and was unable to sleep. She aroused Zech and said, "Will you buy me a horse?"

"Huh?" he responded sleepily.

"A horse, Zech. I want one of my own."

"Sure. What kind you want? A green one or a blue one?"

She shook his shoulder. "Be serious!"

"You want a horse, you got a horse. Would you like a marshtackie, like Ishmael? A little horse would be better for you. It's like riding in a rocking chair."

"I'd love a little horse, but I've never seen another like Ishmael. All the horses at Fort Drum are big, like the ones all the other men here have."

"The Indians have more like Ishmael down in the swamp where they live. Sometime this fall when we don't have much to do I'll take a trip and get one for you."

"Will you really?"

"First chance I get."

"I love you, Zech. You're so thoughtful."

15

The shingles arrived at mid-morning, and by late afternoon the cabin was completed, a day early. That night he and Glenda slept in it, and an hour after dawn the next morning the MacIvey caravan reached the ferry landing, crossed the river and headed east.

They traveled slowly, stopping often in mid-afternoon so the men could hunt deer that would be roasted whole on sweetgum spits over beds of hickory coals. Glenda traded places with Tobias, riding the horse with Zech while Tobias drove the buckboard, Emma disapproving and cautioning Glenda to go easy, but keeping her secret about the baby.

They were five days out of Punta Rassa, turning to the northeast toward the lower Kissimmee, when they entered an area of scrub pine and thick palmetto. Glenda and Zech were riding ahead, with Frog and Skillit at the rear, behind the wagon.

The first shot came from a thicket on the right, striking Glenda's horse in the shoulder, sending it tumbling forward instantly. She tried to jump from the saddle as the horse crashed down on top of her. Zech wheeled Ishmael just as a bullet exploded the horse's brain, peppering him with blood. He too hit the ground beneath the horse.

Tobias stared disbelievingly as Glenda and Zech struggled to break free; then he shoved Emma from the buckboard and jumped on top of her, shielding her from a spray of splinters as bullets ripped into wood. The horse bolted forward, taking the buckboard past the dead horses and directly toward the line of fire.

Pearlie Mae jumped from the wagon and ran for a palmetto clump, dragging all three boys with her, screaming, "Oh my! Oh my!"

Frog emptied his Winchester in less than ten seconds, firing into bushes and palmetto, aiming in the direction of smoke puffs and fire belches. Then he jumped to the ground, struck the horse to make it move away, and started reloading.

Skillit followed Pearlie Mae, making sure she was safely hidden in the brush; then he too fired the rifle.

Zech struggled and kicked, finally freeing himself from the dead horse. He pulled the rifle from the saddle holster and used Ishmael as a shield, lying flat and shooting over the horse, then glancing back and seeing Glenda under the horse. He crawled over the ground to her, untangled her foot from the stirrup and pulled her into the palmetto.

Tobias and Emma also crawled for cover, hopping quickly, leaving the rifle in the buckboard. Then he remembered the shotgun lying in the wagon bed. He dashed forward, grabbed it and a sack of shells, and ran into the brush.

The horse stopped the buckboard at the edge of a thick line of trees. Tobias watched as two men jumped into the wagon bed and struggled with the trunk, sliding it toward the rear. He said to Emma, "It's the gold! They are trying to kill us for the gold! They must 'a followed us all the way from Punta Rassa!"

The buckboard was fifty yards away, and Tobias thought in his mind how much the shots would spread in that distance. He put a shell in each barrel, aimed at the space between the two men, and pulled both triggers at the same time. The gun was loud. Both men screamed as they were knocked backward from the buckboard, killed.

Tobias reloaded the shotgun, waiting for a sign, watching for a puff of smoke or fire to give him direction. He fired one barrel, aimed quickly to the right and fired again, hearing more screams.

The barrel of Frog's rifle became too hot to touch as he loaded and fired again and again, covering the ground with empty shells. He was not even aware of Skillit beside him, also firing rapidly at any sign of life across the open space.

None of them knew the exact moment the opposite firing stopped as they kept pouring lead into bushes and trees; then one by one they lowered their rifles and listened, hearing no sound except their own heavy breathing.

17

Tobias ventured out first, going to the wagon and squatting behind it; then Zech walked to Ishmael and knelt beside him, his face white, shaking the body as if to awaken it. Frog jumped on his horse and charged across the open area, Tobias shouting, "No, Frog! No! Don't go in there yet!"

Frog paid no attention as he galloped full speed into the woods and disappeared.

Emma rushed to Glenda, having seen her go down with the horse, finding her lying in the bushes, clutching her stomach and moaning.

"Glenda? Are you all right?"

Glenda's face twisted with pain as she said, "It hurts, Emma. It hurts real bad. I think I'm losing the baby."

They heard Emma's voice, "Zech! Come here! Get your tent and put it up here! Hurry!"

"They killed Ishmael," Zech said absently, still shocked.

"Forget the horse!" Emma snapped sharply. "Glenda's hurt! There's no time left! Move quickly!"

"What's the matter with her?" Zech asked.

"Stop asking questions and move!" Emma insisted. "Just do what I tell you! I'll explain later!"

As soon as the tent was up, Emma and Pearlie Mae moved Glenda inside. Zech hovered outside, forgetting the dead horse as concern for Glenda pushed all else from his mind. He paced back and forth.

"She lost the baby."

"Baby? Glenda was going to have a baby? I didn't know, Mamma! Why didn't she tell me? I wouldn't have let her come if I'd known!"

"Now don't you start that!" Emma said harshly. "I don't want to hear a word of it! She told me, and I promised not to tell you for the very reason you just said! She kept it a secret because she wanted to come along and be with you and with all of us! She loves you that much! Can't you understand this?"

"I wish she had told me."

"She's the bravest girl I've ever known, and you ought to be proud of her. Now you go on in there, and don't you say one word to make her feel worse than she feels now! Do you understand me, Zech? This is not her fault! She didn't shoot that horse out from under herself!"

Emma put her arms around him and stopped him for a moment. "Oh, Zech. I'm so sorry this happened to you and Glenda. Just don't blame her. It wasn't her fault."

His face was sad as he pulled away. "I'm not blaming Glenda anymore, and I know whose fault it is."

The baby's grave was tiny, the other huge. Zech insisted they bury Ishmael too. Crosses made of hickory limbs were at the head of each mound.

All of the men were soaked with sweat from digging, their shirts dust-covered and clinging to their bodies. Zech held Glenda up, his arm tightly around her, bringing her from the tent although Emma advised against it. Tobias turned to Zech and said, "You want me to say words, or you want to do it yourself?"

"I'll do it myself. It's my baby."

Zech took off the black felt hat and pressed it to his chest. Then the others did likewise. He said, "Lord . . . bless this little baby. Make her to be a fine woman . . . like Mamma and Glenda. Amen."

Then he led Glenda back to the tent and went inside with her.

At Emma's insistence they camped for two more days, letting Glenda rest and regain strength. Zech roamed the woods, finding wildflowers and putting them on the grave each day.

On the third morning they put Glenda into the covered wagon, Emma riding with her and Zech driving. Tobias rode with Skillit and his family on the buckboard.

Zech glanced at the graves one final time; then he popped his whip and moved the oxen forward.

CHAPTER TWENTY-SIX

✟

Seytember passed into October as the men made trip after trip into Fort Pierce, buying and stockpiling barrels to be used when the oranges matured later that year. February's blossoms turned into green globes that grew larger each week and would cover the trees with balls of gold.

Glenda recovered fully, and the nightmare was gradually over-shadowed by the everyday routine of living, not forgotten but looked upon as one more tragedy endured.

It was the end of October when Zech set out alone for the cypress swamp to purchase a marshtackie for Glenda and anoth-er to replace Ishmael. This would be no fun trip, camping often and shooting game along the way. His saddlebag contained smoked beef and biscuits, and he cantered the horse more than he walked it. He was expected back as soon as possible to help with the orange harvest.

As he rounded the eastern shore of Okeechobee and turned southwest, something came back to him that had been pushed far back in his memory, Tawanda. During those years Glenda remained in school in Jacksonville, and he knew he would even-tually marry her, he gradually forgot Tawanda, thinking he would never see her again, or even visit the Indian village.

He wondered if she were still there, if she had married and had children. She was only a memory from the past, and he was not sure he could even recognize her.

He skirted the eastern edge of the custard-apple forest and entered the swamp, searching for something familiar, some land-mark that would jar his memory and point the way, but he found none. It had been too long, and now all trees looked the same, all ponds and sloughs the same, all trails the same.

For two days he wandered, becoming more discouraged as he zigzagged from east to west and moved southward, going deeper into a forest that seemed even more awesome than he remembered, sometimes plodding the horse through shallow coverings of water that lasted for miles before finding firm ground. He was considering giving up the quest when he was confronted by an Indian armed with a rifle.

Zech was startled when the man stepped from behind a palmetto directly in front of him, blocking the way. His eyes were angry, and they both stared silently until Zech said, "I'm looking for the village of Keith Tiger. I've been there but I'm lost now. Can you give me directions?"

The Indian made no answer except to motion with the rifle for Zech to follow him. One hour later they entered a clearing dotted with chickees.

Other than two old women in the cooking chickee, the village seemed deserted. As Zech dismounted, his guide pointed with the rifle but still did not speak. This puzzled Zech, for the reception his father received from the Seminoles had been friendly, so different from this.

He tied the horse to a bush and walked to the edge of the clearing, finding two old men sitting beneath one of the chickees. Again he searched his memory for recognition but found none; then he said, "I'm looking for Keith Tiger. I have business with him."

One of the men said, "I am Keith Tiger. What is your business?"

"You don't remember me, but my name is Zech MacIvey, son of Tobias MacIvey. I was here once with my father."

The old man smiled, Zech's first sign of welcome, making him feel more at ease. "It is good to see you, Zech MacIvey, and you are welcome. You have grown so much I did not know you.

When you were here before you were a boy, and now you return as a man. How is Tobias?"

"He's doing pretty good at times, but he still has spells of malaria. He's not as strong as he used to be."

"None of us are as we grow older. It is a pity of time passing. But I worried about Tobias when he left here so sick. It is good to know he survived. What brings you on such a long journey to find me?"

"I want to buy horses," Zech responded, sitting in front of Keith Tiger. "Two marshtackies, like the one you gave us a long time ago. I didn't know anywhere else to get them but from you."

"They are yours for the asking, but I will accept no pay. We still owe you for the cows you gave us. I will have the horses brought here in the morning. They are at a place deeper in the swamp. We do not keep our horses and cows here in the village where they might be seen."

"Tomorrow is fine, but I'll be glad to pay."

"You have paid already for much more than two horses. Your father is a friend we will never forget. And do not be troubled by your reception here. No one knew who you were, and there has been much trouble lately between our people and some bad white men in the Ten Thousand Islands. It will be different when you are known as a MacIvey. Our people will come back into the village soon and I will tell them. Are you hungry?"

"Yes, I am," Zech admitted. "I was in a hurry to get here and didn't cook along the way."

"Then you must eat now. Come with me and I will get food for you."

Zech followed the old man to the cooking chickee were he was ladled a large wooden bowl of turtle stew and given a chunk of koonti bread. He sat on the ground outside the hut and ate as Keith Tiger returned to the chickee. He thought of asking about Tawanda but decided against it, thinking she no longer lived in the village and was elsewhere with a family of her own. It disappointed him that he would not see her even briefly or at least know what happened to her.

After eating he unsaddled the horse and then returned to the chickee, finding Keith Tiger asleep. He didn't want to disturb the old man so he went back to his horse, mounted and rode bareback into the woods, following a trail to the south. He would like to see Pay-Hay-Okee again but knew it was too far a journey for an afternoon; and even if there were time, he was unsure of the way.

He walked the horse slowly, killing time, feeling uncomfortable alone in the village without even the old man to talk to. He wished the hours would pass quickly so he could take the horses and leave.

The voice came from behind him as the trail turned to the left. "It is you, isn't it, Zech?"

He stopped the horse immediately and looked back, seeing her standing there, the same brown skin and deep-set eyes, the flowing black hair.

She said, "I watched you as you came into the village. Can I ride with you?"

He reached down, took her hand and pulled her up behind him. "Why didn't you come forward and speak? I thought you didn't live here anymore."

"I was too surprised. I didn't think I would ever see you again, and there you were. Why did you wait so long to come back? I watched the trail each week until I finally gave up."

"I wanted to come back, but too many things happened with my family. I thought of you a lot."

"I thought of you too. All the time at first, and then I tried to forget. But I couldn't. I'm glad you're here now."

"There's something I must tell you, Tawanda," Zech said. "I'm married now."

The words did not shock her or anger her. She said, "It doesn't matter. Is she pretty?"

"Yes, her name is Glenda."

"You have not told me why you're here."

"To buy horses. I want marshtackies, and I can't find them anywhere else. I have to start back in the morning and help Pappa harvest his oranges."

His other world seemed far away.

Then they rode into the village together.

The marshtackies were waiting, and after a final farewell he tied them behind his horse. He put a loaf of koonti bread Tawanda prepared for him into the saddlebag, then rode away quickly, not looking back.

As he approached his home in the hammock, he looked back at the marshtackies, the reason for his trip, trying to decide which he should keep for himself and which would be Glenda's. Keith Tiger had selected a stallion and a mare, telling him that marshtackies were becoming rare and would someday soon die out and vanish forever, that if he wanted more he should raise his own from this pair.

He would take the stallion and give Glenda the mare, for the mare would be more loving and gentle. He was sure Glenda would approve of his decision and be happy with the mare, for she wouldn't know how to handle a stallion as well as he.

CHAPTER
TWENTY-SEVEN

🐂

1883

Solomon MacIvey was born March 12, 1883.

They chose the name Solomon because Zech had been reading the Bible and discovered that Solomon, son of David and king of Israel and Judah, was noted for his wisdom. Sol, as they would call him, would be a very wise man indeed, since he would be the first MacIvey to have his own private tutor from birth. Glenda would give him knowledge beyond all things Zech and his father could ever know, and he would be the one to build a MacIvey temple rather than a frontier house made of rough cypress long since turned black by exposure to the weather.

When it came time in April to move the herd for grazing, Emma and Pearlie Mae both refused to go, telling the men to look out for themselves while they stayed behind to look after Glenda and the baby. He didn't like it, but Skillit was elected cook by a vote of three to one.

Zech didn't want to leave home, fearing that in his brief absence the baby would grow up and not know him as the father. He was puffed with pride but would not hold the baby, convinced that such a small and delicate thing would surely break in his rough hands. He cautioned Glenda and his mother to be very careful with Sol, causing them to smile knowingly and assure him they would do their best while he was gone.

Tobias decided not to move the herd too far from the hammock and to send a rider back every two days to make sure the women were fine. They moved south, heading for the lower Kissimmee valley where the marsh and prairie grass should be plentiful.

It was mid-week of the second week when six riders came out of the southwest and approached Skillit on his right. One said briefly, "Who owns these cows?"

"Mistuh MacIvey," Skillit answered, pointing. "That's him over there, just behind the herd."

Zech noticed the riders and came over to see what they wanted. One said to Tobias, "Where you taking this herd?"

"Nowhere in particular," Tobias responded. "Just grazing wherever they want to go. We do it ever summer."

"Well, you can't go any further in this direction."

"How come?" Tobias asked, thinking it was another situation like the one they encountered at the salt marsh. "I don't see any more cows anywhere. "

"This is private land, all the way from here down to Lake Okeechobee. You're trespassing right now."

"Private land? How come all of a sudden it's private land? It's always been open range."

"Not any more. This is Disston land. Mister Disston bought four million acres here."

"How many?" Tobias questioned, baffled by the figure.

"You deef? I said four million. Bought it from the state for a million dollars. Mister Disston has done run all the squatters off, and he's got plans to drain all this land and develop it. He's already got dredges working. He don't want nobody driving cows in here, and that includes you. "

"What if I want to drive a herd through here to Punta Rassa? What could I do if he closes the land?"

"I don't care what you do. You can take them cows slam around the south end of Okeechobee or you can go back north and find another way. But you're not going through here."

"What if I do it anyway?" Tobias shot back, his anger beginning to boil.

"I got a hundred and fifty men working on this place, and all of them are armed. We'll shoot ever cow that enters. Now if you want to convert them cows to carcasses, you just go ahead and push 'em in the direction you're going. That's all I got to say."

With that the men rode off a hundred yards and stopped, forming a line facing the herd, rifles drawn.

Tobias said to Zech, "Go tell Frog and Skillit to turn 'em. We can't fight a hundred and fifty men. We'll go back north and then cut to the west, toward the salt marsh. But ain't nobody got the right to close off the land!"

"Pappa, this is just the beginning," Zech said. "Someday there won't be any open range left. Last time I was over at Fort Drum and talked to Mister Turner he said men are out everwhere now, surveying land for new railroads, and the railroad companies are buying everything they can get. The lumber companies and turpentine men are doing it too. Someday it's coming to an end, Pappa, and there's nothing we can do about it."

"You're wrong!" Tobias responded. "It ain't coming to an end, and it never will. But if this keeps up, we'll just put in more orange trees and run less cows. Prices keep going up like they been doing we ought to be able to clear a thousand dollars a acre on oranges."

"Maybe so, Pappa. But if we stay in the cattle business we're going to have to own the land and fence it too."

"Fence it? That's the best way I know to start a range war. I know what I'd do if I came to a fence. I'd cut it."

"And maybe get yourself killed for doing it."

"Whose side are you on? You sound more like a landlord than a cattleman."

"I'm not talking sides, Pappa. I'll always be with you, and you know it. What I'm talking is sense."

"We'll see," Tobias said. "Go on now and help Frog and Skillit turn the cows. We'll find grass elsewhere. There just ain't no way we can face a hundred and fifty men."

As Zech rode off he thought about the land he had already bought and the deed lying in a drawer in his cabin, MacIvey land that would never be closed to them. He must plan soon to convert more of the gold doubloons into land.

CHAPTER TWENTY-EIGHT

1888

The cattle drives were reduced to one every two years, and much of the grazing was done on MacIvey land. More and more they saw other herds on the prairies, landless men searching for open range and free grass; and often the sound of Winchesters could be heard firing in the distance, warning intruders away. Had it not been for Emma they would have already fought in at least a half dozen all-out gun battles over grazing rights. Others were not so fortunate as range wars broke out everywhere.

Tobias gradually increased his orange grove to three hundred acres, and if they never owned another cow, the grove would provide a good living. But cows were in their blood, especially Zech's, and they refused to give it up. It was a way of life too deeply ingrained to discard easily. The days of driving herds across open land where nothing could be seen but endless wilderness were vanishing rapidly, but there was still profit in cows. Tobias wanted to fight for it, but Zech was making other plans. First he would fence the MacIvey land, which he had increased to thirty thousand acres; then he would look to the south for additional land. The last great manless frontier lay to the south of Lake Okeechobee, and it was there he felt his future lay. Someday he would explore this land.

Skillit left the caravan as they returned from Punta Rassa, telling Tobias he had a "chore" to tend to in Kissimmee. Tobias wondered about this, remembering that Skillit's previous "chore" of finding himself a wife had taken several years. There were now five boys riding in the wagon with Pearlie Mae, and their wailing had been the only sound of babies born in the MacIvey hammock since Sol.

It was just before noon when Skillit came into the clearing, driving a wagon hitched to two oxen, his horse trailing behind. Tobias watched curiously as Skillit tied the oxen and came to the stoop; then he said to him, "Where'd you get that outfit?"

"In Kissimmee. They's good oxen, ain't they?"

"They look right fine, but we don't need another team."

"I jus' thought I wanted 'em," Skillit said, casting his eyes downward.

Tobias noticed that Skillit was not looking at him as he spoke, avoiding his eyes, and this puzzled him. He said, "Are you feeling poorly, Skillit? You don't seem right to me."

"I's fine, Mistuh Tobias. Must be something I et on the trail."

Zech rode up on the marshtackie stallion, which he had named Tiger, and Sol was in the saddle in front of him, his red hair tousled down his forehead. Zech said, "Sol rode Tiger by himself down in the woods, and he did right well for the saddle not to have a horn. I've got to get him a western saddle so he can have something to hold on to. You should 'a seen him go, Pappa. He looked like a frog on a rabbit's back."

Glenda had come outside unnoticed. She said, "I don't doubt that one bit, but you shouldn't turn a five-year-old boy loose on a horse. First thing you know you'll have him branding cows."

"Next year," Zech said, dismounting and putting Sol on the ground. "One more year and he can ride herd as good as anybody. We'll have us another drover."

"I can do it now, Mamma," Sol said excitedly, scurrying to Glenda. "I can ride as good as Pappa."

"Let's see how good you can wash your face and hands," Glenda said. "Dinner's ready. All of you hurry on up before it gets cold."

They gathered at the long cypress table where they still shared common meals, continuing the practice although the clan had grown larger. New planks were added to make the table bigger.

Frog popped a fried pork chop into his mouth and said, "Where you been to, Skillit? I figured you'd done wore pore old Pearlie Mae out an' gone after a new wife. Where you got her hid, out in the woods? Pearlie Mae gone kill you for sure."

"There you go again, Frog, always teasing," Emma said. "And don't talk with your mouth full. It doesn't set a good example for the young 'uns."

"Sorry 'bout that, Miz Emma," Frog answered, "but Skillit sure looks like he's been up to something."

Skillit suddenly pushed his plate away and started sobbing. All of the others were startled, and Frog said in a quiet voice, "What's the matter, Skillit? You ain't never got mad before when we jawed each other. I didn't mean nothin'. I'm sorry."

"It ain't that," Skillit said, his voice choked. "I done a thing I ain't proud of."

"What is that?" Tobias demanded. "I've never seen you carry on so, Skillit. You done killed somebody?"

"Nawsir, it's more than that. I been with you more than twenty years, Mistuh Tobias. You been the onliest family I ever had, but it's time to go now. I got to leave."

"You what?" Tobias asked. "How come you say that? You're family, Skillit. You can stay here as long as you want to."

"I's gettin' old, Mistuh Tobias, an' I got five boys to look to. I got to see to them. I took some of that gold you been givin' me all these years an' bought me some land south of Kissimmee. I got to start my own place so them boys can have somethin' goin' for them after I's gone. I hope all of you ain't too mad at me. It would kill me if you is."

"Nobody's mad at you, Skillit," Emma said, understanding the meaning of the words. "You done the right thing. I'm proud of you."

Tears formed in Tobias' eyes. He was shocked by the news but he understood. Skillit's desire for his own place was the same he had known all his life. He said, "Couldn't nobody be mad at you for what you done. You got a right to do what you want, same as anybody. But I'd like to help. You need more money?"

"Nawsuh, Mistuh Tobias, I got enough. You done give me more than I ever dreamed of. I got plenty left after the land to build me a house an' buy some cows an' hogs an' chickens an' start a little farm too. We'll make do fine. But I done something else you might want to shoot me for."

"It would have to be powerful bad," Tobias said.

"When I went to the land office the man tole me he couldn't record the deed jus to Skillit, that I had to make up a last name if I didn't have one. I put it down as Skillit and Pearlie Mae MacIvey, an' all the boys too. I done took yo name, Mistuh Tobias. If you wants me to I'll go back an' change it to something else."

The shock and grief flushed out as Tobias said, "That's fine, Skillit! We're proud you took the name. You're welcome to it."

"You know what you've done, Skillit?" Emma said. "You've given me six grandsons instead of one. I'm right proud too."

Skillit felt relief that he had revealed his decision without ill feelings. Had the response been otherwise he might have backed away and stayed at the MacIvey hammock. He said, "Lawd, you sho' fine folks! I done got me my own place an' a name too! An' it won't be like we's gone. It's close enough we can come back an' visit whenever we want to. An' if you needs me on a drive I'll go."

"And if you have need of us we'll come," Tobias said. "If anybody hassles you they'll answer to me. MacIvey's stick together, white or black. When you aim to set out?"

"Soon as we get our stuff loaded in the mornin'," Skillit responded.

"Then we'll have a celebration tonight," Emma said. "I'll cook the biggest meal you ever saw."

"If she's gone do that, you ought to come back and leave ever week," Frog said.

Zech listened to it all but said nothing, too many memories cropping up at once. His voice choked as he said, "Y'all excuse me a minute. I'm not sure I tied my horse." He went behind the house and stood there alone, staring at the little cabin where Skillit and Pearlie Mae lived, thinking of all the things Skillit had been a part of, good and bad. Then he washed his face at the stoop and went back inside.

*P*earlie Mae stood by the loaded wagon, crying so hard she could only croak, "Missus Emma . . . Missus Glenda. . . ."

Both hugged her, and then Emma said, "God bless you, Pearlie Mae. We'll miss you."

Skillit gave Frog a bear hug, pressing the breath from him. "Bless you, Frog . . . you old buzzard bait! An' you take care of yo'self. You gettin' old too, like me."

"Ain't no use bustin' my ribs over it," Frog said. "You need me to help out with something you let me know."

Skillit then hugged Tobias and Zech, afraid to say more lest he would unload the wagon and stay. The boys clambered into the wagon bed as he helped Pearlie Mae to the seat. He tried to speak again but couldn't; then he popped the whip, moved the oxen forward and said, "I got to go now. . . ."

The others drifted away silently as Tobias and Emma continued watching the wagon until it disappeared into the woods. Tobias said, "It's breaking up, Emma."

"Yes, it is. But it has to sooner or later. Nothing lasts forever. Everything ends."

"Us too. Our time is coming. But it's sure been something while it lasted."

"It rightly has."

She took his hand in hers and they walked back toward the house, trudging slowing as if tired, Tobias looking down at the deep ruts the loaded wagon cut in the sandy soil.

♦

1892

"**I** wish I could have made Pappa stay at home," Zech said, eating alone with Glenda. "He'll soon be sixty years old, and he's too sick to be out here on the prairie."

"The spells are coming more often," Glenda said, "but you can't tie him up with ropes and leave him behind."

"I will next time if I have to. I'd rather tie him up than see him die out here in a cypress stand."

"Does there really have to be a next time," Glenda asked seriously. "Won't the orange trees make enough money without us driving cows all over the countryside to Punta Rassa?"

"I suppose so. But the whole thing of shipping from Punta Rassa is going to be settled someday. There's trouble brewing in Cuba, and sooner or later there'll be a war down there. When it happens, there won't be any more Cuban market. Someday all the cows will be shipped up north on the railroad."

"That would surely be better than this," Glenda said. "I hope it happens soon. And we've got enough land of our own now to fatten cattle for market. We don't have to roam around out here looking for grass. If you would just go ahead and fence our land we could stay at home until shipping time."

"I'm going to do that, but it'll sure cause trouble with that Allister family up north of us. Every time I go up that way they're on our land. I've warned them but they don't pay any more attention to me than they would a jaybird. They're as stubborn as

Pappa about open range."

Sol came galloping in on Tiger and was followed by a new man Zech hired named Lester. He was in his early forties and a typical cracker drover, rail-thin, beard-covered and somber, like Frog. But also like Frog, inside he was both gentle and tough when he had to be.

Sol was stamped from his father's mold except for the red hair. He was already taller than most boys at age nine, broad-shouldered and lanky. He said, "Is Grampy feeling better?"

"I suppose," Glenda responded. "We'll be moving on soon, so you and Lester better eat now."

"I'll see to Grampy first," Sol said, bounding off toward the wagon.

Tobias was sitting beneath the shade of a palmetto, mopping his forehead with a damp cloth. His hair and beard were now completely gray, his body even leaner than ever. Sol threw his arms around him and said, "How you feeling, Grampy? You missed a good one this morning. We saw a bear over by the edge of the woods, and when I charged toward him with Tiger he ran away."

"I seen enough bears already," Tobias said. "But you best be careful. There was a time when a bear would snatch you off that horse and eat you, and then eat the horse for good measure."

"Here, swallow this," Emma commanded, shoving quinine into Tobias' mouth.

Tobias frowned, then he said to Sol, "Boy, don't ever let yourself get into the mess of having a woman around always shoveling medicine into you. It ain't worth it."

"Hush up and go eat!" Emma snapped. "You get more cantankerous every day. You're worse than an old billygoat. You need food for strength."

"See what I mean," Tobias said, smiling. "She's like a crow sittin' in a tree, squawking at everything that passes."

"You can ride in the wagon with Granny if you want to," Sol said. "Me and Pappa and Lester can handle the cows. I could do it by myself if they'd let me."

"I suppose you could," Tobias said, getting up. "You're a MacIvey through and through, for sure. And I might just ride with Granny for a day or two and let you prove yourself."

"That's the only thing you've said that makes sense," Emma said. "You don't need to be out there in the sun on a horse. Them cows can chomp grass without you staring at every bite they take."

"We'll do it!" Sol said enthusiastically. "We'll handle the cows while you rest up some. But come on now, Grampy, and let's eat! I'm about to starve."

Tobias took the boy's hand and felt himself tugged hurriedly toward the cooking pot.

Emma smiled at both of them as she followed.

The herd grazed in a northwesterly direction, eleven hundred cows, mostly homegrown rather than popped wild out of swamps. By not driving to market each year the calves were given time to grow on land closer to home. Some were still rounded up wild but not so many as in days past.

One morning they could see the railroad in the distance as the sun reflected off shiny steel rails. It was the new line into Tampa. Zech and Frog had come upon a section of it under construction while scouting grazing land, and the foreman contracted with them for delivery of two dressed steers each day for forty dollars per steer. They followed the workers for over a month, killing and dressing beef at the corral and taking it to the site in the wagon. When the construction crew moved too far away for the dressed meat to be transported safely in the heat, they followed the crew for two more weeks, driving cows with them and butchering on the spot. Then they left the project and returned home.

When the lead steer reached the rails they could see smoke boiling up on the horizon, painting a black streak in the sky. Soon afterwards a tooting sound broke the silence of the prairie.

The cows poured halfway across the rails and stopped, oblivious to the engine puffing toward them. Zech and Frog popped their whips frantically, trying to move the balking herd.

Tobias jumped from the wagon and watched as the train came closer without slowing, and then he shouted, "That fool is going to plow right into 'em!"

Zech and Frog wheeled their horses and got out of the way as the engine smashed into the herd, its iron cowcatcher scooping up three cows, crushing and killing them instantly. The train then came to a stop a hundred yards down the rails.

Zech looked at the mangled bodies; then he and Frog rode quickly to the idling engine, its stack belching soot over the grass. Zech shouted, "What do you mean, fellow? Can't you see a herd of cows a mile away? If you'd stopped that thing, we'd 'a got them out of the way!"

The engineer leaned out the window and shouted back "If you hadn't 'a had them yellowhammers on company property it wouldn't 'a happened anyway. You're going to make us late!"

"That's no excuse for what you done!" Zech said angrily. "The railroad's got no right to keep us from passing. You know that as well as I do. You could 'a stopped for a few minutes. Who's going to pay us for the cows you killed?"

"File a claim with the headquarters office in Tampa," the engineer said. "But don't try to charge us a hundred dollars each for buzzard bait worth fifteen. We won't stand for it no more! I ain't never seen so many hundred dollar cows till we hit some flea-bit varmint out here on the prairie, then all of a sudden it's worth its weight in gold. Who do you crackers take us for anyway, a bunch of fools?"

None of them noticed Tobias as he walked on the side of the engine, carrying the shotgun. He aimed at the boiler and pulled both triggers, blowing an eight-inch hole in the steel plate. Steam shot out and hissed loudly, like angry rattlesnakes, spewing a white cloud over the engine.

The engineer and the fireman hit the deck as Zech and Frog's horses bolted away. Tobias lowered the shotgun and walked calmly back to the wagon.

The engineer finally peeked out the window and said, "What do you think you are doing?"

Zech brought the bucking horse under control and returned to the edge of the billowing steam cloud. The engineer jumped from the cabin and came to him. "Do you know what the old fool has done?" he shouted. "It'll take us a half day to patch the boiler and get up steam again! Who's going to pay for this?"

"We'll swap out," Zech said, trying hard to be serious. "We'll trade you our dead cows for your hole. That ought to about even things up. We'll see you. And good luck with the patchin'."

As Zech and Frog rode off the engineer shouted after them, "Idiots! Crackers!"

Zech made no comment to Tobias as they moved the herd on across the tracks and to the west. Frog rode up to him and said, "The old man's still got fire in his guts, ain't he?"

"Sure seems that way," Zech said. "That breech loader has killed everthing but a train engine, and now it's done that too."

After crossing the railroad they turned due north and grazed for a week; then one morning another herd was spotted on the horizon. Wishing no trouble, Zech ordered them to move south again. They recrossed the rail line without incident and drifted to the southwest.

At noon one day a week later they were once again approached by armed riders. Off to the right of the herd, no more than two miles away, Zech could see men digging frantically with both

machines and shovels, cutting wide gashes in the earth. As soon
as the riders reached him he said, "What's happening over there?
It looks like the biggest fishbait digging contest I ever seen. Must
be some kind of worms them fellows are after."

"Tain't worms," one man said. "It's phosphate. You'll have to
turn away. There's no way you can get them cows through here,
and it's the same slam over to the coast and for fifty miles south.
You best go east and around."

"Appears to me they're just digging up dirt," Zech said, puzzled.
"How'll they ever get all them holes filled back up?"

"They won't. As I said, it's phosphate. Folks has gone plumb
wild over it, as bad as the forty-nine gold rush. Speculators are
jumping around like rabbits, buying land and filing claims and
jumping claims and shooting at each other. If I were you I'd cut a
wide path away from here afore some fool cracks down at you
from behind a bush. The mine over yonder belongs to a company out of Chicago, and they aim to fence the whole area. We got
orders to turn everbody away."

Zech felt no anger as he had when they were denied entrance
to the Disston land. He said resignedly, "I guess you're just
doing your job. We'll cut east and find another way to Punta
Rassa. But it sure seems the whole prairie is going crazy. I
don't know what use they'll ever make of them big holes once
they're done with the mining."

"Beats me, but I think nobody cares. I'm paid to ride guard, and
that's all. I ain't in the hole business. But if I were you, mister, I
wouldn't come this way again. We done had two gun battles this
week over that stuff they're digging up, and there's four men dead
'cause of it. You best stay away."

"I'll do that," Zech said. "And I thank you for the advice."

They turned the herd eastward for several days, and then
south again, finding land that seemed like times gone by, endless
stretches of palmetto prairie and scrub pine shared only with
herds of deer and flights of birds.

One night as Zech listened to the lonesome cry of a wolf, realizing it was a harmless lone voice and not a pack, he wondered what the future held for old enemies like wolves and bears and for all the other creatures that depended on the land for survival. He remembered that night years ago when he had witnessed the ritual of animals peacefully sharing the life-giving water, some inborn instinct telling them they must share and conserve to survive. Perhaps animals are smarter than men, he thought, taking only what they need to live today, leaving something for tomorrow. Even the hated wolf kills only for food and only for immediate need. Maybe it is man who will eventually perish as he destroys the land and all that it offers, taking the animals down with him.

As he thought of these things and the unknown future, he realized one thing was certain: if the wilderness shrinks, pushing more and more men together, there will be explosions without end. Some will yield but others won't, and someone will be hurt. It will never be like the animals sharing water.

🐂

After they had bought cows from several small ranchers, the herd numbered two thousand when they reached Punta Rassa at the end of the summer. The market price had gone up to twenty dollars per head, and Zech collected forty thousand dollars in gold doubloons. Tobias was not present when the accounting was made.

After loading the gold on the wagon, Zech went into the office of Jacob Summerlin, the present owner of the Punta Rassa shipping facility. He said to him, "I'm interested in buying some land south of Okeechobee. Is there a land office down there anywhere?"

"There's a small trading post on the southwest shore," Summerlin replied. "Mostly does business in 'gator hides and egret plumes, but the man who owns it is a land agent. What you gone do, go in the bullfrog and wildcat business? I don't know why anybody would want a piece of that place."

"Oh, I don't know, Mister Summerlin. I went through there once a long time ago and just thought I'd like to have some of it."

"I imagine you can get all you want. Most folks don't even know where it is, but there's beginning to be activity over that way. There's some commercial fish houses dealing in catfish, but they're mostly on the north shore and the east side. I don't know of a thing to the south."

"Last time I went there from Punta Rassa, we followed the river to the lake and then turned south. It seems that's pretty far out of the way if I'm heading straight for the south shore. Is there a better way to get there?"

"Well, if you go straight east from here you'll run into a place called the devil's gardens. If you go in there, you're liable not to come out again. Some folks claim it's haunted. Past that is another swamp just about as bad. If you swing down south from here don't go too far in that direction. That's outlaw country. I wouldn't go in there with nothing less than General Grant's army. Best thing to do is follow the river again for about thirty miles and then turn southeast. If you ride steady you can make it in a day more or less, depending on how good your horse is.

"Thanks for the information," Zech said. "I'll see you next drive we make."

As he walked away Summerlin shouted after him, "Hey, MacIvey! Don't let nobody down there sell you a 'gator farm!"

Emma suggested to Zech it would be wise to let Tobias rest at the cabin for a week before setting out on the return trip, and it was during this idle time Zech contemplated making the trip to Okeechobee.

When he arrived at the cabin, he called Glenda aside to discuss what he intended to do. He said to her, "If we stay here for a week I'll have nothing to do but sit, so I thought I'd ride over to Okeechobee and see about buying some land. Mister Summerlin told me where to go. Would you mind being here without me?"

"No, I don't mind at all. We'll be fine. How much land are you thinking of buying?"

"I don't know. I'll stuff both saddlebags with doubloons and buy whatever I can get with it. We may never need land down there, but again we might. And I'd rather have the land than more gold sitting in trunks back at the house. We'll pretty soon have to start storing it in the barn."

"How long do you think you'll be gone?"

"I'm sure I can make it there and back before we start home. I'll leave at dawn tomorrow and take Tiger. He'd be faster on a trip like this than the roan. Whatever time it takes, I'll be back as soon as I can."

"Don't kill yourself or the horse by hurrying. There's no need

43

of that. It's good for Tobias to rest for as long as we can keep him here. I sure hope you can talk him out of making any more of these trips."

Zech cantered the marshtackie for two hours at a time and rested him when they encountered thick woods, then cantered again. Moving steadily without stopping to eat, he covered the sixty miles to the lakeshore and found the trading post before sundown.

The owner was a relatively young man of forty, dressed in blue overalls and brogan shoes. He seemed mildly surprised when Zech entered the store. "Kinda late to be pushing a horse way out here," he said. "I don't see many riders near to sundown. Where you coming in from?"

"Punta Rassa. I've been riding steady all day. You got some cheese?"

"Nope, sure don't. It's too hot here to keep cheese. I tried it once and it spoiled before I could sell it, a whole fifty-pound block. Turned plumb green. I gave it to some Indians and they et it anyway. You didn't ride slam over here from Punta Rassa for cheese, did you?"

Zech ignored the question. "What've you got to eat? I didn't have room in my saddlebags to bring food."

"Tinned beef. How many you want?"

"Two cans will do for now."

He took the meat from a shelf, handed it to Zech and said, "Where you headed? You sure don't smell like a hide trader. If the wind's blowing this way, I know when they're coming when they're still ten miles away."

"Right here. I'm interested in buying land and was told you're an agent."

"Yeah, that's right, I am. But it's just a sideline. My main business is trading. If I had to depend on the commission I get for handling land sales in these parts, I'd 'a starved to death a long time ago. What keeps me in this place is 'gator hides and egret plumes. Them feathers is bringing two bucks each now. Ain't that something? Two bucks for something growing out of a bird's rear. What you interested in?"

"Land to the south of the lake."

"How much you got in mind? It comes in eighty-acre sections. You want a whole section?"

"How much is it an acre?"

"Going price right now is fifteen cents. But as I say, you can't buy no less than eighty acres. Anything less than that ain't worth my time to make the deed. I've had fellows come in here and want to buy five acres to put a cabin on. Can you imagine me going to the trouble of making out a deed and recording it for seventy-five cents?"

"You got a pencil and a piece of paper?" Zech asked.

"Sure. But I can tell you right off what a section is worth. It's twelve dollars."

"I'd like the pencil anyway."

Zech figured for a moment, scratching his head along the way. He rechecked his figures and said, "I want sixty thousand acres."

"Would you repeat that again?" the man said, staring with deeper interest at Zech.

"Sixty thousand acres. Way I figger it that's nine thousand dollars."

"Well, you figger right. But listen, fellow. We don't sell no land on credit. You got to pay at least half down and the rest in a year."

"I'll pay cash. I've got nine thousand in gold in my saddlebags. I'll bring it in now."

Zech went to the horse, came back and threw the bags on the counter, creating a dull thump. "You can count it whenever you want. It's all there. When can you get the deed ready?"

"For a chunk that size it'll take me the best part of a day, and I'm ready to close up now for the night. My missus don't like to be alone with the young 'uns after the sun goes down on account of all the riffraff we got around here. I can have everything for you first thing day after tomorrow. Does that suit you?"

"It does if it's the best you can do. I hoped to start back right away, but I'll kill the time somehow."

"You pretty good at counting katydids? If you ain't, I can loan you a fishing pole."

"Don't worry about me. I'll be here day after tomorrow."

"Here's a receipt for your money till it's counted and the deed is done," the man said, handing Zech a slip of paper. "Come on over here and look at this map on the wall. It shows the whole general area, and you can point out where you'd rather have your land."

Zech studied the map for a moment; then he put his finger to it and said, "Right in there to the southeast will do fine."

"That area is the best of the lot," the man said, marking it with a pin. "It ain't all swamp like some of it. I'll make sure the description is right for whenever you want it surveyed."

"I'd appreciate that."

The man took a ring of keys from a nail and said apologetically, "I'd ask you to stay the night at my place but we don't have no spare room at all."

"That's all right. I'll be fine."

"Lordy me!" he then said, popping his fingers. "You shook me so with that land order I plumb forgot to ask your name for the deed."

"Zech MacIvey. And I want three names on it, my wife and boy too. I'll write it down for you."

The man accepted the printed names and said, "I'm Jasper Thurmond. It's been a pleasure doing business with you, Mister MacIvey."

"You too," Zech responded, turning and leaving the store.

He mounted Tiger, rode a short distance to an oak tree, dismounted and opened one tin of beef. As he ate hungrily, he wished he had brought Sol along just for company. After finishing the beef he built a fire, spread a blanket and fell into a tired sleep.

At dawn Zech ate the remaining canned beef and washed it down with water from his canteen. For a while he watched the rising sun burn the sky and tint flights of egrets heading out over the lake; then he lost interest and mounted the horse.

At first, he rode south aimlessly, bored already with waiting for the deed, not at first aware he was heading in the direction of the Seminole village. Realization came slowly as he plodded onward, and then he calculated he was no more than twenty miles from the village. It would be a good day's outing and something to do while killing time, and also a chance to see Keith Tiger again.

He had not thought of Tawanda when he planned the journey to the south shore of the lake, so close to her and the village. The purchase of land had been his only reason for coming. It had been too many years, too many happenings, and surely she would be married now with children of her own. Perhaps he would at least be able to speak to her briefly and learn her fate since their last meeting.

This time he did not become lost and wander vainly as before, hoping to be discovered rather than discover. On his last trip he studied the landscape carefully, making mental notes in case he ever did return; and now when he saw changes from meadow to slough to swamp he knew the direction he wanted to take.

He reached the village at noon and found it to be the same as the last time he rode in, deserted except for two old women beneath the cooking chickee. No one challenged him as he approached. He tried to talk to one of the women but she couldn't understand him, making signs toward the south of the clearing and chattering in a tongue unknown to him. Then he looked into all of the chickees and found them empty.

He sat on a palm stump, trying to decide what to do, to wait longer in hopes of someone returning soon, or leave now and reach the trading post before nightfall. Then he was startled as a marshtackie ridden by a young boy bounded out of the brush, dashed full gallop a yard from him and disappeared into the woods.

Several people then ran into the clearing as if chasing the horse. One of those people was Tawanda. She stopped suddenly in front

47

of him, staring wide-eyed.

"Zech? Zech? Is it really you? I don't believe it!"

"Yes, Tawanda, it's me," he replied, getting up. "I almost got run over by a horse just now. Who was that boy flying through here on the marshtackie?"

"It was my son, Toby. The men are breaking horses at a corral in the swamp and we've all been watching. Toby rides well, doesn't he?"

"I'll say. That horse barely touched the ground going by here. He rides like the wind. You must be real proud of him."

"Yes, I am."

He was still as surprised as she, and for the first time he looked at her, seeing that she was as he remembered, not yet touched by the years, still youthful with sparkling eyes and flowing black hair.

For a moment more neither of them spoke, as if waiting expectantly for the other to make the first move, and then Tawanda said, "What are you doing here? I still can't believe it's really you."

"I had some business at a trading post on the south side of the lake and just decided I'd try to find the village. This is the first time I've been back down this way since that time I came for the marshtackies."

"It's been over nine years, Zech! I think I can truthfully say that you don't visit very often."

As they talked, Tawanda told Zech that the boy on the horse was really their son, born of their Indian marriage.

"I've had a son all this time and didn't know. What can I do for him? I'll do anything you say."

"Do for him?" she questioned. She thought for a moment, and then she said, "Yes, there is something you can do for him. You can promise me you'll never interfere in his life. Never! In no way. You must let him grow up here among his people where he's happy and where he belongs. He will never be a part of your world and you must know this, and you must never tell anyone in your world about Toby. Do you promise, Zech? This is all I ask of you."

"If that's what you want, I promise. I'll never interfere, and I'll never tell anyone. But I wish I could do more."

"When he comes back, you must meet him. After that, I'll fix food for the three of us. Would you like that?"

"Yes, I would. I would very much like to know Toby."

A marshtackie digging its hooves into the dirt stopped in front of them. Toby jumped down, ran to Tawanda and said excitedly, "Did you see it, Mother? He's the best of the lot! I'll keep him for myself!"

"Yes, I saw," Tawanda said, trying to calm him. "But forget the horse for now. There's someone here you must know. This is your father, Zech MacIvey."

The boy wheeled around quickly and stared at Zech, his eyes wide and boring into the stranger. Zech tried to smile but couldn't, and then he said, "Hello, Toby. It's good to know you. You're a fine-looking boy, and you ride as good as anyone I've ever seen."

"You really think so?" Toby said, unsure of himself and what to say or do. "Would you like to ride the horse?"

"Yes, but not now. I'd like to be with you first. Tell me about yourself. What do you like to do best?"

"Ride horses."

"It was the same with me when I was your age. I rode a marsh-tackie too, and his name was Ishmael. He was given to us a long time ago by Keith Tiger. He was killed, but we have two others like him. One of them is tied over there."

Toby glanced across the clearing at the horse. "What's his name?" he asked.

"Tiger. I named him after Keith Tiger."

"You named him for a Seminole?"

"Yes, and I'm proud of it. The Seminoles have always been our friends. And I want to be your friend too."

"Will you go hunting with me?"

"I'll do anything you want me to do. And I have presents for you. Wait right here and I'll get them."

Zech walked quickly to his horse and returned carrying the Winchester and a hunting knife with a nine-inch steel blade. He handed them to Toby and said, "These are for you."

Toby's eyes widened again as he turned the rifle over and over in his hands. "You mean this is for me? I can keep the rifle and the knife as my own?"

"They're yours now. And before I leave I'll teach you to shoot the rifle. It's loaded, so be careful with it."

Toby put the rifle down and ran to Zech, throwing his arms around him. He said, "Thank you, Father! I've never had such presents!"

Tawanda watched both of them, and when she heard the word "father" she smiled. Toby turned to her and said, "Can I go now and show the rifle and the knife to Billie Bird? He won't believe what I have unless I show him!"

"Yes, go and show everyone you wish, but come back soon. We'll all eat together."

Zech smiled too as the boy bounded off, shouting, "Billie! Billie! Come see! Come and see what my father brought me!"

Tawanda said, "You have made him very happy, Zech. He never expected to own such things. But wasn't it foolish to give away your rifle and face the return trip unarmed?"

Zech thought of how little the rifle now meant to him except as a killing tool, and how much it seemed to mean to Toby, the same feeling he had when Tobias first gave it to him. He was also touched by the proud shout, " . . . what my father brought me!" He finally said, "It doesn't matter about the rifle. I have a pistol in my saddlebag. I hope I don't need a gun. But there's something you maybe can answer for me about this trip. A man at Punta Rassa warned me not to go too far south coming here, that it's outlaw country. Do you know anything about this?"

All traces of a smile disappeared quickly as Tawanda said, "Yes, I know. We all know. There are very bad men in the area of the Ten Thousand Islands. They have sugar cane fields there, and they keep slaves, white men they capture. They keep them in chains and work them like oxen. One of our men was held like this but managed to escape. They also go out and roam the land, stealing cattle and driving them back there. Some they slaughter, and others they take by boat to Key West to be sold. They have killed several of our men and boys who wandered too close while hunting or fishing, and they think no more of killing a man than a snake. I have warned Toby to never go that way."

"Could be they're the same ones who attacked us and have stolen our cattle. How many are there?"

"No one knows for sure."

"Well, I'd like to wipe them off the face of the earth, and some-day I will."

"Don't be foolish, Zech!" Tawanda exclaimed with alarm. "Never go there! If you do, you may not return. My people know that instant death awaits anyone who comes too close to those men. Please, Zech, do not even think of what you have said!"

Tawanda's seriousness startled Zech, and he wished he had not asked the question. He said in a calming voice, "Let's just forget that I even asked, Tawanda. I'll go back the same way I came, far to the north of them."

"When do you have to leave?" Tawanda asked, relieved that Zech apparently dismissed the subject from his mind.

"The deed to some land I'm buying will be ready in the morn-ing, and I'd planned to leave as soon as I pick it up. But I'll stay here tonight and tomorrow so I can spend some time with Toby. One more day won't make any difference in getting back to Punta Rassa."

"We'll enjoy the next two days together, the three of us."

When he reached the trading post and picked up the deed, he didn't purchase even one tin of beef for the return trip. Instead, he put Tiger into a steady canter and headed non-stop for Punta Rassa.

It was just past noon when the MacIvey caravan crossed the Kissimmee below Fort Basinger and turned north. Although Tobias had gained strength and seemed normal, they stopped early each day on the return trip for him to rest. The closing days of summer were the hottest of the year, and Emma fretted that the prairie heat would bring back the chills and fever. And there was no need to hurry. The orange crop wouldn't be ready for harvest for two or three months and there was little to do until then.

They stopped an hour later at the edge of a large hardwood hammock and made camp in the cooling shade of a live oak. All but Tobias and Emma rode away to hunt deer or turkey for the evening meal.

Emma built a fire and put the cast-iron pot over the flames, getting ready to cook. If the hunters failed to bring back wild game, she would make her usual stew of smoked beef and potatoes. There would also be biscuits and hot coffee. Frog alone could drink a quart with each meal.

Tobias spread a blanket at the base of the tree and fell asleep. He would have preferred to follow the others but he needed a nap.

Emma peeled the potatoes, put them into a bowl and covered it with a cloth to keep out the flies; then she kneaded the biscuit dough, rolled it on a cypress plank and patted it into little round mounds. This too she covered and set aside, waiting always until the stew or roasted game was done before putting the dough into the Dutch oven for baking. Tobias liked his biscuits fresh from the oven and piping hot, and she always tried to please him.

After these chores were done she decided to go into the woods and pick the last of the season's huckleberries for a special treat of pies. This was usually done by Glenda but on this afternoon Glenda wanted to go with the men on the hunt.

The tiny berries were now fully ripe and deep purple, and most of the bushes had been raided by birds. She picked several bushes clean of all the remaining berries, and they barely covered the bottom of the wooden bucket; then she moved on to find others. Some she plopped into her mouth and ate, staining her lips with the sweet juice.

The sun-blocked darkness of the deep hammock felt good to her, cooling her as she moved, and when she reached the river-bank the berries were four inches up the side of the bucket. One more inch and there would be enough for four pies.

She turned south and picked along the bank, soothed by the rippling sound coming from the river, enjoying this brief moment of quiet.

Time passed swiftly, and finally she realized she must start back to the camp. She had gone but a hundred yards from the river when the pain hit her, causing her to stumble and fall to the soft ground. She tried to get up but could not do so, and then it came again, a searing hot flash that burned into her chest like a branding iron. At first she was too stunned to realize what was happening to her, and then she knew. Her only thought was that she was going to die alone in the woods without once again seeing Tobias and all the others.

Sweat poured from her face, and when she wiped it away with her hand, she discovered that her flesh had no feeling. For several minutes she lay on her back and looked upward into the trees, her eyes on a squirrel that squatted on a limb and barked at her.

She finally forced herself to a sitting position but could not rise further.

Her will to return to Tobias proved strong, and she struggled to her feet and walked shakily. She stumbled, falling and then righting herself, stopping often to lean against a tree trunk, step by step making her way back to the camp.

Tobias was awake now, and when she staggered from the woods he took one look at her and screamed, "Emma! . . . Emma! . . . What is wrong with you?"

She said feebly, "The pain, Tobias . . . it hurts so bad. . . . It came on me sudden. . . ." Then she wilted and fell to the ground.

Tobias ran to the buckboard and snatched up his whip, popping it three times; and then he fired both barrels of the shotgun. He rushed back and dropped down beside her, his heart pounding so wildly it formed a tight ball of spit in his throat. He gagged as he put his hand to her forehead and wiped sweat from her eyes, and then he said, "Emma. . . . Emma. . . . Don't you leave me, Emma. . . . You hear me! . . . don't you leave. . . ."

She looked up at him, her eyes momentarily clear; then her hand went to his. She said, "Tobias . . . Tobias . . . I'm sorry. . . ." Then the last flicker of life went out of her.

Tobias shook her, gently at first and then violently, crying, "Emma! . . . You can't do this. . . . Emma! . . . Emma! . . . "

He was not aware when Zech rode in and jumped from the horse, taking one look at the lifeless form and then shouting, "Pappa! What has happened? Did someone do something to Mamma?"

Tobias sat by the body, shocked speechless, swaying back and forth as he chanted, "Emma. . . . Emma. . . ."

Zech grabbed his father's shoulder and demanded, "What has happened, Pappa? You've got to tell me! Did those bushwhackers do something to Mamma?"

Tobias finally looked up and said, "No, Zech, it wasn't that. . . . It was her heart . . . or maybe she was just wore plumb out from this hard kind of life. . . . I don't know . . . but she's gone from us, Zech, and it ain't fair. . . . It just ain't fair."

"Oh Lord," Zech moaned as he dropped to his knees beside his father.

Glenda cooked the potatoes Emma had peeled, knowing the men should eat, but the food was ignored. Zech took Tobias off alone and said to him, "Pappa . . . you want to dig the grave now?"

At first Tobias made no answer, as if his thoughts were elsewhere and he didn't hear the words; and then he said, "We'll not bury Emma out here alone on the prairie. We'll take her back to the hammock where she belongs."

"The heat, Pappa," Zech said. "We're several days from the hammock. . . . The heat. . . ."

Tobias suddenly snapped awake and said, "I don't care about the heat! If I have to I'll shoot every buzzard along the Kissimmee River! Emma's going home, Zech! We'll not stop till we get there! Do you understand me?"

"Yes, Pappa. I understand. We'll leave right away and not stop till we reach the hammock."

Zech went back and wrapped Emma in a blanket, then he and Sol placed her in the wagon. Glenda helped Tobias onto the buckboard seat, and as soon as all were mounted, Zech said to Frog, "You and Lester ride on ahead of us and build a coffin. Make it of cypress, not pine. And have it ready time we get there."

"Yessir, Mister Zech," Frog responded, grief-stricken too, his tired eyes dripping sorrow. "We'll do that, and we'll make it good. It's got to be a fine coffin for Miz Emma."

Zech then popped his whip, moving the oxen and the horses forward.

By traveling steadily and as fast as the animals could be pushed, they reached the hammock at nightfall the next day. The coffin was waiting, and Tobias directed it to be placed on chairs in the main room.

Glenda removed Emma's clothes and bathed her with damp cloths, and with Zech's help, they dressed her in the blue dress she had worn but once at the wedding. After placing her in the coffin, Zech removed the bottle of perfume from Emma's dresser drawer and poured it over the body.

Glenda came back into the room and said, "What is that smell, Zech? It's gone all over the house."

"Peach blossoms. Mamma always smelled good to me, and now she does again. It's what she would have wanted."

Tobias sat at the table, statuelike, as he gazed absently across the room, getting up and looking into the coffin and then sitting again. Zech suggested that he sleep, but he would have none of it, refusing to leave even for a moment.

Zech went to his cabin and lay down, bone-tired, but he couldn't sleep. He went back to the house and sat by his father in the dim glow of the coal oil lamp.

Tobias turned to him and said, "You know something, Zech. It was your mamma who held this family together when times was roughest. Hadden been for her you and me would 'a probably starved. She could cook pine tree roots good enough to keep a man alive. And I never did nothin' for her. With all the gold in them trunks I could 'a bought her fancy dresses and shoes and such as a woman likes, but all I ever gave her was that cook stove. And now it's too late to do anything. I waited too long."

It bothered Zech that his father was feeling guilt about Emma, and he said, "She didn't want stuff like that, Pappa. It wouldn't have meant anything to her. All she wanted was to be with us and help out all she could, and you made her as happy as she could be. She told me that several times when me and her talked. She loved you, Pappa. More than anything."

"She told you this?" Tobias questioned. "You really heard her say it?"

"Many times, Pappa. Me and her used to talk a lot before I got married, like a mother and a son. The kind of talk me and you couldn't do. It's the truth, Pappa. I swear it."

The words soothed Tobias, and he said, "I'm right beholden to you for telling me now. I was afeared she might have held it against me for keeping her out here in the wilderness. But you listen to me now, Zech, afore you have cause to regret it. Don't ever take a woman for granted as nothing more than a cook. I should 'a done a lot for Emma, but I didn't. And it wasn't because I didn't love her. I did that truly. But I put it off and let it slip my mind till now it's too late. Don't make the same mistake, Zech. If you do, it will pain you more than any varmint can ever hope to do. It pains me now just as much as that awful thing that struck down Emma, only I'm still here to live with it and she ain't."

"I'll heed your words, Pappa. But don't you ever worry none about Mamma being happy. She was. She was the most happy woman there ever was. Now why don't you go in the bedroom and get some sleep? I'll be right here with Mamma."

"I'll rest after Emma is at peace in her own ground. Not till then, and maybe not ever. So don't waste your breath by askin' me again, Zech. I ain't going to budge from here till the sun comes up. This is the last night I'll ever get to spend with Emma in the house and I intend to make the most of it."

As soon as daylight came the grave was dug. Glenda greeted the returning men with a hearty breakfast of fried pork, grits and biscuits, but it seemed eerie to all of them sitting at the table without Emma's bustling smile as she went from table to stove and back again. Tobias refused food altogether, taking only coffee as he glanced constantly at the crude coffin resting just ten feet from the table. It was still impossible for any of them to accept the fact that Emma would never again occupy the chair that now sat empty beside Tobias.

As soon as they finished eating he closed the coffin lid and nailed it shut.

Ground fog hazed the clearing as they came outside, Zech, Frog and Lester carrying the coffin with Tobias, Glenda and Sol following.

This was Sol's first encounter with death and it frightened him. Tears were mixed with sheer horror as he looked at Emma for the last time before the coffin was closed, seeing his beloved Granny lying still and unable to speak, knowing in a boy's own way that he would never again feel her warmth and strength as she put her arms around him and whispered just for the two of them alone, "I love you, Sol." And now as the procession moved slowly to the grave, he hovered close to Glenda, holding her hand and trying desperately not to break down and cry like a child in front of the others.

They put ropes around the coffin and lowered it into the awaiting earth; then Tobias stepped to the foot of the grave. For a moment he bowed his head in silence, and then he said in broken words, "The Good Book says the Lord giveth . . . and the Lord taketh away . . . but this time, Lord, You done took back an awful lot. We ain't been no churchgoin' folks like we ought to, but it was because there wasn't no church to go to out here in the wilderness where You directed us. But Lord . . . there ain't never been no finer woman put on earth than Emma. I thank You for the time we spent together . . . and I wish You had let her stay here with me longer. I'll miss her powerful . . . and I don't understand why she had to go 'stead of me. I don't think it's fair, but that's Your judgment . . . but take her to You with the same love she had when she was here. Amen."

At this point Tobias stopped, then he spoke again softly, as if the words were meant for Emma alone: "Emma. . . I say to you truly. . . you may be gone in the flesh. . . but you'll always be right here with me. . . always. I love you, Emma. . . and happy sailing . . . ."

Zech had never heard his father use the saying before. It surprised him, but he knew the meaning. He echoed, "Happy sailing, Mamma. . . ."

Tobias threw in the first shovel of dirt; then he stood by and watched as the grave was filled. Long after the others had gone back to the house he was still there. He had not changed positions when Zech came back an hour later and placed a bundle on the head of the grave, a large bouquet of white pond lilies, wild white roses, wild yellow senna and purple deer tongue.

CHAPTER THIRTY-TWO

✝

1894

For over a year Tobias grieved, seldom leaving the clearing and having no interest in cows or anything. After this period of mourning he gradually focused his attention back on the orange grove, his one personal pride and satisfaction, and he spent most of his time there, often just sitting alone among the trees. Zech often said that Tobias counted each tiny orange as it changed from a blossom, knowing in advance exactly how many barrels the crop would fill. And this was more fact than jest.

Zech, Glenda and Sol moved into the main house to be closer to Tobias, and Glenda assumed all of the chores that once were Emma's, the cooking and washing and housecleaning, never complaining or asking for help. Several times Zech offered to hire someone to come live on the place and help her, but each offer was refused. Whenever the men were tending herd close by, she went out each day in the buckboard with a hot meal for them, and often she rode horseback alongside Zech and the others as they drove cows into the corral for branding. Zech could not remember the last time she wore a dress, seeing her daily in the jeans and chambray shirt and the wide-brimmed black hat. Without the flaming red ponytail hanging down her back, she could have passed for just another cowhand.

Zech and the men started fencing the MacIvey land, going to Kissimmee and bringing back wagon loads of barbed wire, cutting cypress posts in the swamp and stringing the unfamiliar barrier yard by yard across the open range, coming back week after week and finding it cut, then stringing again. He knew this would eventually lead to trouble, but he was determined to see it through.

There had been no drive to Punta Rassa in two years, and this was the reason Zech wanted to fence the land. He planned to raise his own herds, give up the practice of wandering with them all summer, and fatten them on MacIvey land before driving them to market; and there was no way to contain the cattle except with the hated wire.

They were still bothered constantly by rustlers, often finding cows killed on the range or driven away. During the previous summer they took turns riding armed guard both day and night, but it did no more good than looking for invisible sand flies. The raiders were indeed ghosts, killing and stealing and then vanishing. Only now, Zech felt sure he knew where they were coming from. His thoughts turned more and more to the Ten Thousand Islands area.

Zech also remembered the things Tobias said to him the night before Emma's burial, and each time he went into Kissimmee or Fort Drum or Fort Pierce he brought back gifts for Glenda, dresses still hanging unused in her closet, ribbons and bottles of perfume, aprons with lace borders—all of them useless on a wilderness homestead but nevertheless appreciated by Glenda. His mother's death and Glenda's willing assumption of Emma's role brought them even closer together, forming an unbreakable bond between them.

December 28

"Pappa! Come down off there before you sail away like a kite! The wind's too strong for us to pick any longer!"

Tobias paid no need to Zech as he continued to perch on top of a wooden ladder leaning against an orange tree, a canvas sack slung over his shoulder.

Zech shouted again, "Pappa! Come on down before I come after you!"

"I'll finish the sack first!" Tobias shot back. "Go on about your business and let me be!"

"Stubborn old billygoat," Zech mumbled as he walked away and started loading filled barrels onto the ox wagon.

Glenda's special Christmas dinner with roasted turkey and mincemeat pies was still fresh on everyone's mind as they put the holiday behind them and worked the grove. There was a bumper crop of juice-filled globes, and the harvest was about a third finished.

The wind started early that morning, and the sky far in the north was totally black, signifying a coming northern. This was the time of year when brief storms and cold fronts rushed across the land and then disappeared as quickly as they arrived, making the temperature go up and down rapidly, often changing as much as thirty degrees in one hour. It was not a thing of dread but something to look forward to, not only for its temporary cooling effect but also because it sweetened the winter crop of collards now full grown in the garden and made the oranges even juicier.

Everyone else went back to the house as Zech waited for his father to finish picking and empty his sack into a barrel. As soon as this was done he drove the oxen to the barn and stored the barrels inside the adjacent orange shed.

By mid-afternoon the wind got much stronger and roared instead of growling. It lashed the hickory and oaks and popped the palmetto as the temperature dropped sharply, causing Zech to shiver as he left the house and went to the small corral attached to the rear of the barn. Frog and Lester were already there, driving the horses and oxen inside where they would be given a feeding of hay and bedded down for the night.

Frog pulled the lightweight denim jacket tighter around his

neck and said, "Feels like the devil's stingin' me. This storm gone be a humdinger if it gets much colder. I think I'll build a big fire in my cabin. That ought to keep a old man like me warm."

"I guess it would," Zech said. "But before you do that we need to chop more firewood."

By the time Zech got back to the stoop, the outside thermometer attached to the wall showed only three degrees above freezing. He brought an armload of stove wood into the kitchen and returned for another, and in this short time the mercury had dropped to thirty-one degrees.

Tobias was sitting close to the stove when Zech brought in the last load of wood. "How's it doing out there?" he asked.

"Getting colder, Pappa. It just went to a degree below freezing."

"If it keeps this up and holds for long, it'll sure hurt the oranges. I wish we'd got done with the pickin' before this came."

"It'll probably ease up and pass by. It always has. If the wind keeps up like this it'll blow the cold over the tops of the trees anyway. There's no need for worry."

"Maybe so," Tobias said doubtfully, "but if the temperature drops much more, everbody better pray it don't rain. If it does, we'll have an ice storm like you never seen. I seen it happen a many a time in Georgia when I was a boy, and it always started out just like this."

"Well, it didn't really hurt nothing, did it, Pappa?"

"Not so much that nature didn't cure in the spring, but we sure didn't have orange trees up there."

At suppertime the kitchen was cozy-warm, and the meal took on a festive air. After a sweltering summer and the sultry dog days of early fall, a cold snap was a welcome relief. It thickened the blood and invigorated everyone to a point of exhilaration. No one except Tobias seemed to be particularly concerned as the wind pounded the side of the house and rattled the cypress shingles.

Frog helped himself to a second portion of collard greens and corn pone and said, "If it's still cold in the morning we ought to go out and shoot wild hogs. There ain't no better time for the killin' and dressin' of hogs. It makes the meat taste sweet as honey."

"That's not a bad idea," Zech agreed. "We could cook some fresh, smoke some and salt down the rest. We might could get enough pork to last all winter."

"Can I go too, Pappa?" Sol asked, excited by just the mention of a hunt.

"This time you can. If you're not old enough now to face a wild boar you never will be. Way before I was your age I'd done killed a bear with Pappa's old shotgun."

"That's for sure," Tobias said. "Zech done it when we lived up in the scrub. Two bears tried to get in the barn one night when I was off driving Confederate cattle up to Georgia during the war. When they hemmed your granny up, Zech blowed one of them bears slam across the clearing and into the woodshed."

Sol's eyes widened as he said, "Really, Grampy? Did Pappa really do that? You're not funning me again, are you?"

"He sure enough did."

"Will you tell me about it sometime? Please, Grampy, will you?"

"I'll tell you about it when we ain't got nothing better to do. So just hush up about it now. And I'll tell you a lot more besides that. We seen some things and done some things folks nowdays wouldn't believe."

"Would you believe your big brave daddy tripping over his own boots and falling flat on his face at a square dance?" Glenda said to Sol.

"Did you do that, Pappa?"

"Can't say as I did," Zech laughed. "Leastwise, I don't remember. But your mamma once ate some rattlesnake meat and threw up all over the prairie."

"That's enough!" Glenda snapped. "Not at meal time anyway. We started out talking about hog hunting, so how did we get around to all this?"

"Well, Miz Glenda," Frog said, "when you get a bunch of dodo birds perched on the same fence, like they is in here now, there ain't no telling which way the conversation will go. But getting back to hogs, are we goin' in the morning or not? If we ain't, I won't come out at sunup and freeze my tail off for nothin'."

"We'll go," Zech said. "Come first dawn we'll eat and leave."

"Not me," Tobias said. "My days of chasin' some scrawny varmint all over the woods is long gone. I'll stay here and help later with the scrapin' if you get anything to scrape."

"Fair enough," Zech said, relieved that Tobias did not want to go. "We'll meet here in the kitchen at dawn."

Before going to bed Zech stoked the fire to keep the room warm during the night; then he took the coal oil lamp and went out to the stoop. The wind made the flame flicker and nearly go out as he held the lamp in front of the thermometer. It now read twenty degrees, a temperature drop of fifty-five degrees since morning, and for the first time he shared Tobias' concern. But he learned long ago they were all powerless and at the mercy of their most fickle and deadly enemy, the weather. It couldn't be shot or hanged or roped or corralled or harnessed in any way. It made them helpless, and whatever was to come would come, regardless of worry or concern. He glanced once more, and then he turned and went back into the house.

*D*awn was late in coming because the sun couldn't get through a low covering of black clouds boiling just over the treetops. There was an eerie gray gloom over the clearing when Zech came outside and looked at the thermometer. It read fourteen degrees, and the cold slapped into his face like ice water. He shivered violently and went back into the house.

He went to the stove and backed up as close as he could get to it, shivering again, feeling the heat tingle his flesh as it drove away the cold. Glenda put on the coffee pot and said, "What's the reading now?"

"Fourteen degrees. The water bucket is froze solid. If it wasn't for the wind still blowin' we'd be knee deep in frost. I've never seen it so cold."

"Are you still going hunting?"

"I guess. It's up to the others. If they want to, I will, but we'll all have to wear two pairs of britches."

"It's foolish to go out in this. You'll make yourselves sick."

"Well, if we do go, I don't think we'll have to shoot any hogs. They'll be so froze we can pick 'em up like cord wood and bring 'em on back to the house."

Tobias came into the room and poured himself a mug of coffee. He said, "I heard what you said, Zech. Fourteen degrees. That means the oranges are gone. And if it holds for much longer, the trees'll go too."

Zech knew the truth of this, but still he didn't want Tobias upset. He said, "Don't count them out yet, Pappa. This may blow over by noon. If it does I don't think it'll leave much damage."

"If you believe that you also believe a jaybird can play a fiddle."

There was nothing more Zech could say, and he was relieved when Frog and Lester came into the house and interrupted the conversation.

Frog backed up to the stove and said, "Lord have mercy. What a feelin' it is to drape your bare bottom over one of them outhouse holes on a mornin' like this! I think my butt is froze solid."

Glenda smiled and shook her head as she continued the task of making fried hoecakes for their breakfast. She mumbled, "You men!"

After the meal was finished they took the rifles and went to the barn to saddle the horses. The cold rushed through the double layers of clothing like they weren't there, burning the skin and making the bones feel like they were being crushed. If any one of them had backed out the others would follow gladly, but no one made the suggestion, each waiting to see what the others would do.

Zech said, "Any hog with good sense is going to be buried as deep as he can get in some bushes. I don't think we'll have much luck without dogs, 'less we riot them out ourselves."

"Well, I ain't goin' to stick my foot in no bushes for sure," Frog said. "They'll be rattlers in there too. Maybe we ought to just ride for a spell and see what it looks like, if the horses don't freeze under us."

"Me and Sol'll go down by the garden and cut north. You and Lester go west. If you need help pop your whip."

"It may be too froze to pop," Frog responded. "And if I'm stuck to the saddle when we get back I'll just ride my hoss into the kitchen."

The horses blew white clouds of icy breath as they trotted away. When Zech and Sol reached the garden they paused and looked over the split rail fence. All of the plants were flat on the ground and had taken on the death color of yellow. Only a few hardy collards were still upright, but the fringes of each leaf were curling. Tomatoes, beans, squash and peppers lay in lifeless heaps.

They turned north and rode into the grove. Zech dismounted, picked an orange and cut it in half with his hunting knife. The inside was solid ice, and when he squeezed it a blob of frozen juice plopped to the ground and bounced like a steel ball. He knew now the remaining crop was a total loss, and he dreaded telling Tobias.

From the grove they went into the creek bottom and found a flight of twenty Carolina parakeets dead on the ground, all frozen. One remaining bird was on a tree limb, swaying drunkenly. As they watched, it fluttered to the ground, flapping its wings in one last desperate gasp of life, and then it too lay still.

The sight of the colorful bodies dotting the ground in motionless heaps saddened Sol. He said, "Pappa, are they all going to die?"

"I suppose so. They can't stand this much cold. It'll kill a lot of fish too, and other things."

Sol then said, "Pappa, I'm not trying to back out of the hunt if you want to keep going, but ever time my hand touches metal it sticks to it. It feels like it's going to pull my skin off. I don't think I can hold my rifle and aim it without some gloves."

"I'm having the same trouble. We best go on back to the house now. There's no need for us to stay out here and freeze for nothing."

Shortly after they reached the house, Frog and Lester returned too. The rest of the day was spent in the room by the stove.

The cold lingered on for two days as they all huddled inside for warmth. A clear sky and brilliant sun greeted the third morning, and the temperature rose rapidly to seventy-five degrees.

Tobias and Zech went to the grove and found the trees not green but brown, each already surrounded by piles of fallen dead leaves. Tobias cut into the trunk of one and said, "It ain't dead all the way. They just might make it if it stays warm like this. I just thank the Lord we didn't get no rain and ice with all that cold."

"They'll make it, Pappa. We may never have another cold snap that bad. What I need to do now is replant the garden. There's not a single thing left in there alive, and I sure don't want to go back to eating wild poke two meals a day."

"Poke ain't so bad. We lived off it for years when we had to."

"I know, Pappa. But tomatoes and beans and collards is better. Soon as we get back to the house I'll put out the seeds."

A month later Tobias came running through the woods, shouting as loud as he could, "They done it! They done it!"

Everyone poured out of cabins and house, and Zech scrambled

from the barn and raced to meet his father as he came into the clearing. He said, "What in the world is all the shouting for, Pappa?"

"The orange trees," Tobias panted, "they're puttin' out sap and new growth! They're goin' to bloom, Zech! They done made it!"

"That's great, Pappa! Just great. I knew they'd come through."

"I sure thought for a while it was all gone, but the Lord's done smiled down on us. I got to go now and tell Emma."

Zech stood by Glenda and put his arm around her as they watched the frail body lumber across the clearing toward the small plot of ground bearing Emma's grave.

February 6, 1895

ech was in the garden, driving thin stakes into the ground beside the tomato and bean plants that were thrusting up from the soft soil, when he felt the first rush of cool air. It was a moist breeze, not hot and dry, and he said to Sol who was working close by, "Goin' to rain soon. It'll be good for the garden. We better hurry and get done with this."

A thunderhead formed in the north, layer upon layer of black clouds that spread rapidly and soon covered the horizon. The wind then came in gusts, blowing leaves from the nearby woods and scurrying them across the garden.

Rain was just beginning to pelt down when they reached the clearing and ran for the stoop. Zech stood there for several minutes, watching the blue sky disappear as clouds raced to the south like galloping horses, turning early afternoon into twilight.

The rain came steadily all afternoon, pattering against the cypress roof, and when Zech finally left the house and ran for the barn to tend the livestock, there was a strange coolness in the air and the rain. It felt like little drops of ice rather than water.

Shortly after dark the wind increased to a howling fury, rattling the windows and making the walls creak. The temperature dropped rapidly, and they put more wood into the stove to warm the room.

Tobias paced back and forth, his face creased with worry. He said to Zech, "I don't like the sound or the feel of this. It's more than a rain storm for sure."

"Don't go seeing buggers in every cloud," Zech said. "You're just gun-shy, Pappa. There's just no way we're goin' to have another storm like that last one. It'll pass over before the sun comes up."

"Don't never say 'no way'," Tobias warned. "Whatever the Lord wants to do He'll do. And He's not goin' to ask our advice about it." The wind didn't let up, and Zech could hear it continue pounding throughout the night. When he crawled from beneath the warm quilts at dawn he was greeted by a room as cold as ice.

He dressed hurriedly and rushed outside, and what he saw stunned him. The temperature was at eleven degrees, and what had been rain the day before was now sleet. Every tree was ice-covered, and the ground was one solid sheet of ice.

Zech and Sol brought in as much wood as they could pile in the kitchen, and the frozen wood made loud hissing sounds as it was put into the fire.

At mid-morning the sleet stopped, and an hour later snow came, a blinding, swirling blizzard that erased the earth and turned the clearing and the woods into a sea of white.

Sol was fascinated, seeing such a sight for the first time, not realizing it was also the first glimpse of snow for all except Tobias, and he had not seen it now since leaving Georgia almost forty years before.

Tobias again paced the room. He went to a window and looked out, frowning as the flakes hit the ground and froze immediately, piling deeper and deeper. He turned to all the others in the room and said, "The Lord's done treed us for sure this time, like a wildcat with no place left to go but down, and the ground full of dogs. There ain't nothing what can survive this. It's all gone now."

Zech did not even try to console Tobias this time, knowing full well his father spoke the truth. Nothing would survive, not even some of the small animals with a covering of fur.

As the day wore on, the air was filled with cracking sounds that came like thunder as overburdened tree limbs gave way from the weight of ice and crashed to the ground. In late afternoon Zech and Frog fought their way to the barn to feed the horses and oxen, and Zech could see that the woods were becoming impassable from cluttered limbs. There were great raw gashes on trees where limbs had broken away.

They had been caught by surprise without enough chopped wood, and in order to save what they had, Frog and Lester left their cabins and came into the house, sleeping that night on blankets spread on the kitchen floor.

The next morning the snow still came, not a blinding blizzard as the day before but a steady falling of white flakes. At noon it stopped and was replaced by sleet once more, frozen rain that formed a hard crust over the seven inches of powdery snow. The thermometer rose only one degree to twelve and hovered there.

There was no festive mood in the house this time, no laughter as they looked out windows at the ice-encased earth, wondering when and if it would ever stop. It was an almost impossible challenge to slide and stumble to the barn and give each animal a short ration of hay. The outside pile of the precious fodder was now a frozen mass made useless.

Tobias went out to the stoop constantly, looking anxiously at the thermometer and coming back inside, repeating the cycle again and again until finally Zech warned him that all he was accomplishing was turning cold air into the house, icy gusts that did not go away without adding more wood to the fire.

Just before nightfall Zech and Frog and Lester went into the yard and brought in more wood, almost exhausting the supply, each dreading the possibility they might have to go into the woods

71

and chop a fresh supply from the ice. Tobias insisted that he help, and in spite of Zech's protests, he brought several loads to the stoop, turning his thin hands blood red and making them sting like fire.

It was when Glenda put supper on the table that Tobias was first missed. All of them paid no heed to his absence from the kitchen, thinking he had gone into his bedroom to rest after helping with the wood.

Zech went for Tobias and found the room empty. He came back into the kitchen and said anxiously, "Pappa's not in there. Did anyone see him come back in the house after the last load of wood?"

"I wasn't paying any mind to him, Zech," Glenda said, becoming frightened too.

"I saw him after that," Sol said. "He was putting some pine kindling into his coat pockets. But I didn't see him no more."

"Oh my Lord!" Zech moaned. "He's slipped out and headed for the grove. I'll go after him."

"I'll go with you, Pappa," Sol said, scrambling for his jacket.

"No! There's no use for but one of us to freeze. I'll see to it myself. The rest of you stay here."

Zech went down the stoop and paused for a moment, letting his eyes adjust to the darkness, then looking ahead at the ghostly forms of ice-covered trees. He made his way forward one cautious step at a time, sliding over the hard crust, entering the woods and moving gingerly through a jungle of shattered limbs, hoping that no more of them would come crashing down and land on top of him. When finally he reached the outside edge he could see it ahead of him, a fire glowing like a beacon, giving him direction to the edge of the grove.

Tobias was standing there, trying to warm himself as smoke and flames leaped upward into the shriveled tree, his frozen beard glistening with ice. Zech emerged from the darkness and said harshly, "Pappa! What do you mean coming out here? It'll be the death of you!"

Tobias turned to him and said calmly, "I had to come here, Zech. I've got to save at least one tree, and heat from a fire is the only way. If I don't save one tree there won't be nothin' left to take cuttin's from and start the grove again. I've got to save one tree."

"Forget them trees, Pappa! After this is over we can grow another tree somehow, but we can't grow another you! Come on now and let's go back to the house before we both turn into chunks of ice!"

"I'll not leave here and let the fire go out!" Tobias said. "Don't you understand what I'm doing, Zech? There won't be one tree left standing nowhere, not here or anywhere! Can't you understand? I'll not . . ." The fire went out of his eyes and the words stopped as his lanky body suddenly folded and toppled backward into the small circle of slush caused by the heat of the crackling pine.

"Oh, Pappa . . . Pappa . . ." Zech said as he picked him up, surprised by how light the frail form was. Then he went back into the darkness, toward the clearing.

Tobias' flushed face poured sweat as they put him into the bed and covered him with quilts. He came awake and said, "You got to promise me something, Zech. You'll replant the trees. Oranges is the best way to go. Better than cows. Don't have to chase 'em. You got to promise."

"I promise, Pappa. Just be quiet and get some rest. We'll talk about it later."

He drifted away again as Glenda put her hand to his forehead and said, "He's burning up with fever. I'm afraid he's got pneumonia as well as a malaria spell. He's real sick, Zech. Real sick."

"I know . . . I know it, Glenda. He may not even last out the night. If I'd known he'd do something foolish like this I would have nailed the door shut. You'd think them trees are the only things on earth that count."

"Maybe they really do mean that much to him."

"Maybe so, but they're not worth this. It's just that when a old man gets something on his mind there's no way to make him let go of it. No way! But he sure did what he thought he had to do. You can't fault him for that."

Zech and Glenda both sat with him throughout the night, Glenda bathing his face with damp cloths, trying to bring the fever down, Zech just sitting and staring, feeling helpless and useless. At daybreak Glenda went back into the kitchen and prepared breakfast.

Sleet still came down from a gray sky, and Zech did not even bother to go out and look at the thermometer, knowing what it would say without seeing it. The windows were now frozen over, making the rooms almost as dark as at night.

Glenda went into the bedroom to lie down and rest while Zech watched Tobias. Everyone else sat by the stove, stone-faced, afraid even to ask what was happening behind the closed door.

Just before noon Tobias became conscious again. He looked up at Zech and smiled, and then he said, "Did you keep the fire goin'?"

"Never mind the fire, Pappa. Just keep still and you'll feel better. You'll be fine soon."

"I ain't goin' to be fine, Zech . . . and I know it . . . and I don't mind none at all . . . so don't fret. It's been a long trail but I'm done with it now. And you know something, Zech . . . I ain't tryin' to run down Glenda. . . . She's a fine woman and a fine cook and I truly thank her for all she's done for us . . . but I ain't had a biscuit like Emma's since she left us. . . . Maybe Emma's got a cook stove up there with her and she'll make me a batch. . . ."

Tears came to Zech's eyes as he said, "Just hush up now, Pappa, and don't talk like that. You're going to be fine. Glenda will make you some biscuits for supper."

Tobias drifted away again; then he snapped back and said, "We done some things, didn't we, Zech."

"Yes, Pappa, we done some things. We surely did."

His eyes then turned upward, staring right through the cypress roof, remembrance flooding from them as he smiled and said again, "We done . . . some things . . . Zech . . . you and me . . . . We done . . . some . . . things. . . ." The voice trailed off as the tired body went limp and lay still.

"Oh, Pappa . . . why'd you have to do it? . . . Those trees!" Zech sat on the edge of the bed for several minutes, physically and mentally stunned, feeling that a part of him had died also. Then he touched the eyelids and pulled a quilt over his father's face.

When he came into the kitchen his sad look said it all, and no one had to ask. Glenda came to him immediately, put her arms around him and said, "I'm sorry, Zech. So sorry. We all loved him."

Sol jumped up and ran into his room, shutting the door so no one could see as he dropped down on his bed and sobbed, "Grampy . . . Grampy. . . ."

Frog sat still. "They ain't never goin' to be another like him," he finally said. "Not ever. Ole Skillit would sure like to know. I'll go an' fetch him when the sleet lets up."

Zech poured himself a mug of coffee and sat at the table. He stared at the steam rising upward, drifting like summer fog from a swamp at dawn. He said to Glenda, "You know what one of the last things he talked about was? Mamma's biscuits."

"Would you like something to eat?" Glenda asked. "You haven't had a bite since yesterday."

He suddenly felt a tremendous need to be alone. Without answering he put on his coat and went outside, walking silently toward the grove, not feeling the cold or hearing the crunch of ice beneath his feet.

Every tree was now dead, killed right down to the ground, forlorn and foreboding in the somber gray glow, a brown sea of death replacing what had been lush green foliage and golden globes. Sleet piled up on his hat and shoulders as he looked down at the black stain, all that was left of Tobias' futile fire. He picked up a piece of half-burned wood and sailed it high into the air, as far as he could throw. It crashed down into the top of a tree, causing frozen leaves and fruit to shoot outward and scatter across the snow.

He said, "Don't you worry none, Pappa. I'll put it all back." Then he turned and walked away.

The next morning the sleet stopped, but the sky was still overcast. The three-day storm left far more damage than any of them yet realized.

Frog saddled his horse and rode away alone to inform Skillit, insisting he could move steadily and return by the next day. Zech worried that he wouldn't make it at all through the ice and snow, but he didn't protest. It was a thing Frog was determined to do and would attempt regardless of any warning against it from anyone. And the delay would cause no problem since the grave couldn't be dug in the frozen ground. It would have to thaw first.

Zech walked into the woods beyond the garden, awed by the strange silence, hearing not one bird call to another or one animal move. The only sign of life he could find was a lone robin perched on a bush, its breast feathers puffed into a red ball.

He stopped several times and kicked at lumps in the snow, uncovering the frozen bodies of rabbits and raccoons and foxes. Then he went back to the barn and measured cypress planks stored in the loft. There would be enough for a coffin, and he would build it himself that afternoon.

When he returned to the house he sat at the table, silent again until Glenda joined him. He said to her, "It's down to just you and me and Sol now, and from what I've seen out there so far, we're back to where this family was twenty-five years ago. I hope there's a few rabbits and coons still alive, 'cause it might be all that's left to eat. We'll have to grub for it again, Glenda, and it's going to be a long time before we get over this."

"We'll make it, Zech. We'll do whatever we have to do."

"You know something else," he said, reaching out and touching her hand. "All that gold we got in those trunks can't be stewed or fried. It's not worth anything unless I can find supplies. And everybody who's got a dime in cash is going to be out buying everything they can find in the way of food. Rations is going to be real short, so as soon as all this ice goes away, I better hightail it to Kissimmee or sommers and get all the flour and cornmeal I can find. If it's all gone time I get there, I hope you know how to cook cattails."

"I'll cook whatever I have to, even rattlesnakes if it comes down to that. We'll make do. But you ought to go to Fort Drum first. Pappa will let us have whatever he can spare. Then you can try elsewhere."

"That's a good idea, and I'll do it." Then he got up and said, "I think I'll go back out and gather up some of the frozen animals. I can smoke 'em and store the meat away. We may have need of it."

Soon after he left the house the clouds cleared and the sun came through, reflecting a brilliant, blinding glare and causing ice to crack from limbs of trees. It crashed down thunderously, preventing him from entering the woods again to gather the carcasses. Like the digging of the grave, the gathering of meat would have to wait until the sun won the battle and thawed the earth and woods.

*F*rog made good his vow, and before noon the next day he came into the clearing, leading the ox wagon through what was now a sea of slush. After a round of greetings and hugging and no small amount of tears on the part of Skillit and Pearlie Mae, the men went to the south edge of the hammock to dig the grave beside that of Emma.

They first raked away the remaining snow, and then they dug

into the mushy ground, spade by spade of dirt thrown aside until the proper hole was formed. It looked so final to Zech that he walked away quickly when the task was finished.

Frog and Skillit helped Zech dress Tobias in his one black suit, complete with white shirt and string tie. They all could not help but remember the time they forced him to put it on for Zech's wedding, threatening him with all sorts of dire things until he finally retired into the wagon and then emerged looking like an itinerant preacher. The suit had not been worn since.

As soon as they placed him in the coffin Zech nailed it shut, wanting all of this to end as soon as possible, also knowing that Tobias would not want it dragged out any more than necessary.

After reaching the grave and lowering the coffin, Zech stepped forward to say last words. This was a new duty for him, and he was unsure of himself. He spoke slowly, "Lord, bless Pappa . . . and see to it he's with Mamma again, where he wants to be. Since You seen fit to take both of them away from us in such a short time, You ought to at least do this. Pappa was a good man, Lord. I never knowed him to do a bad thing . . . not ever. I'll be hard put to measure up to him, but give me strength to try. And one more thing, Lord . . . please don't throw nothing more like this at me anytime soon. . . . I don't think I can stand any more for a while . . . Amen."

Skillit, Pearlie Mae and the boys moved into their old cabin for the night. When they all gathered for supper, Zech at first sat in his usual place; then at Glenda's urging, he moved into Tobias' empty chair at the head of the table. He did it reluctantly, feeling like an intruder, and then he realized he would have to assume the position either now or later. It was a thing he had to do, just as Glenda was forced into the position of Emma. There would be no more Tobias or Emma to take responsibility and lead the way. It was now up to himself and Glenda alone.

They made small talk, remembering things past, things long forgotten—all of them trying to brush death from their minds.

Skillit told of the success of his farm and ranch, pleasing everyone by the news, and the conversations went on for an hour; then tiredness hit all of them and they went to bed early.

Final goodbyes were said just past dawn; then the two oxen pulled Skillit's creaking wagon across the slushy clearing and along the trail leading northwest past the orange grove.

🐂

$\mathcal{Z}$ech made trips to Fort Drum, Fort Pierce and Kissimmee, finding the land devastated everywhere, trees downed, prairie grass dead, cypress stands filled with the decaying bodies of animals. Only buzzards profited from the freeze.

News drifted in from north and south, and Zech learned that orange groves were almost totally destroyed everywhere. Not one tree was alive north of Lake George, and trails leading north out of the state were filled with steady streams of families leaving the land and heading into Georgia or Alabama or the Carolinas or wherever else they could go and start a new life. On his trips he saw long trails of ox carts and wagons going north past Fort Pierce and Kissimmee, loaded with only the things the families could carry along.

He also learned that the one place the freeze didn't destroy was a small village at Fort Dallas, at the extreme end of the eastern coast. It was said orange trees could be bought there for cash, and it was there he would seek trees to rebuild the MacIvey grove.

Food supplies of all kinds were short everywhere, but he managed to buy enough flour to see them through the rest of the winter. Another month and spring would come, turning the woods and prairies green again, and things should improve. But for all those people who were leaving their homesteads, there was no hope and no future. Without cash money there was no way to buy food or replace orange trees or plant new gardens or do anything but pack up and leave, taking with them bitter memories of the great freeze and of what might have been. Those who were lucky enough to get anything at all were selling homesteads they had owned for fifteen or more years for one Spanish doubloon or whatever else was offered, even a sack of cornmeal to eat along the way.

It was six weeks after the freeze and the burial of Tobias when Zech was at the corral, helping brand what few cattle the spring roundup produced. The cows were scattered worse than he had ever seen them, going for miles in search of anything they could eat, and there was hardly a calf left alive. Those that survived the ice storm were killed by packs of hungry wolves as well as bears and panthers. Wolves even got in the corral one night, killing and dragging away a steer. It seemed to Zech that all of the creatures had gone mad, driven to a bloody frenzy by the ice and snow. But he did not mind them taking a steer now and then, knowing they too must eat to live.

Zech was pressing the branding iron to a half-starved cow when he noticed people coming from the south. At first he thought they were just another family heading north, but as they came closer, he could see they were not. There were no wagons or carts, and all of the people seemed to be adults.

He continued to watch until he saw they were Indians; then he mounted his horse and rode out to meet them. Leading them was Keith Tiger, looking like a mummy on a horse. The old man was now beyond age, his white hair capping a face as gnarled as a cypress knee.

Keith Tiger raised his hand in salute, and then he said, "It is good to see you again, Zech MacIvey. You look more like your father each time we meet."

There were thirty men and women in the group, some mounted but most walking. Zech searched them quickly, seeing that Tawanda and Toby were not among them. He said, "It's good to see you, Keith Tiger. But what are you doing way off up here with so many of your people? Are you leaving the land like so many others are doing?"

"We have come to pay last respects to Tobias."

"You've come all this way to do that?" Zech said, surprised and puzzled. "How did you even know about Pappa's death?"

"We learned of it at the Okeechobee trading post, and word was left there by a man who deals in oranges at Fort Pierce. It saddened our hearts to hear of it. Tobias was our friend, and this is what we wish to do."

"You're most welcome," Zech assured the old man. "Pappa would be real pleased. He thought a lot of you and all the others. I'm glad you've come."

"If you would show us the grave now we would thank you. We will camp nearby for the night and leave in the morning. You and I can talk later."

"I would be honored to do that. Just follow me."

Zech led the caravan to the house and across the clearing, past Glenda's curious glances and into the oak grove where the graves were located. He said, "Pappa's grave is the one on the right."

Keith Tiger dismounted and said, "You will leave us alone now if you will. We wish to do this in our own way."

"Take all the time you want. I'll come to your camp later."

As he rode back to the house to tell Glenda what was happening, he glanced back and saw Keith Tiger break a lancewood spear in half and place it on the grave; then he heard chanting, a wailing, mournful sound that chilled him as it grew louder.

As Zech rode through the oak grove he saw gifts scattered over the grave, a pouch made of deer hide, a carved wooden steer, a piece of alligator hide and a cluster of egret feathers. The broken spear was placed across the head of the grave.

He continued through the woods until he came to the campsite. Keith Tiger was sitting on a blanket, eating sofki and beef jerky.

CHAPTER THIRTY-THREE

Zech dropped down in front of him as he said, "Would you join me in food?"

"No, thanks. My wife will have supper ready soon. You're welcome to join us if you want to."

"We have enough with us, but I thank you. We have brought you a sack of koonti flour. We thought you would have need of it. Since the freeze we have sold great amounts of it to the trading posts. People are hungry everywhere. The storm did not hurt us so much as it did to the north. "

"It was bad here, and I appreciate the flour. We can sure use it. If you want I'll round up a few steers for you to take back with you. They're real scrawny, but maybe you can fatten them up."

"We have no need of them at this time. The rifles Tobias gave us have provided food. I hate to think what would have happened to our people without them. And we are still getting calves from the cows you and Tobias drove to our village many years ago. We will never forget all you have done for us."

"Well, I'm sure you can use some bullets. I've got several cases of them stored in the house. I'll bring you a case later this afternoon."

"That would be appreciated. It would take much koonti for us to earn a whole case of bullets."

Zech then got up and said, "I'll come back and talk more in a few minutes. I'd like to visit around some."

Keith Tiger looked at him knowingly as he walked away, a sudden sadness coming into his face. He watched until Zech reached the cabbage palm where Tawanda's father and mother were sitting; then he turned his eyes away.

Zech dropped down to the blanket and said, "I came to ask of Tawanda and Toby. How are they?"

At first the man made no answer, avoiding Zech's eyes, and then he said, "Tawanda is dead, Zech."

The words dumbfounded Zech, shocking him. He said in disbelief, "Dead? Tawanda is dead?"

Tears came into Zech's eyes.

The man put his hand on Zech's shoulder and said, "We believe that one who dies in sadness can never rest easy in the afterlife that comes to all of us. She would not want you to be sad. The last words she spoke were, 'When you see him again, tell Zech I leave this life in happiness.'"

"What of Toby?" Zech then asked. "What has happened to him?"

"We have taken him as our own. We did not bring him here because Tawanda would not wish it. He is a fine young man. Someday you should come and see him again. He has never forgotten your last visit, and he speaks of you often with much pride."

"I'll do that," Zech said, getting up. "I promise you I will, and you tell him so. I must go and speak again with Keith Tiger."

Zech walked back to Keith Tiger and said, "I'll go to the house and get the bullets and take the koonti flour to Glenda. She'll be real pleased with it."

The old man looked deep into Zech's eyes and said, "You know now what happened, my son, and I am sorry it had to be. We are glad a part of you is Seminole. Do not forget this, Zech MacIvey."

"I won't forget. And I'm proud that Toby is my son. It's just that so much grief has come to me lately."

Zech tied the sack of flour to his saddle, and as he rode away he thought of Tawanda and Toby, seeing again the joy in her heart just from his being there with them. He also remembered her saying that he should never grieve for her or for Toby, no matter what came their way. He vowed to himself he would see Toby again.

🐂

CHAPTER THIRTY-FOUR

*N*ature slowly heals itself, and a warm June sun and gentle rains once again splashed the forests and prairies with green.

The men of the MacIvey hammock spent two months clearing the orange grove, chopping down dead trees and burning them in great piles, then pulling lifeless stumps from the ground with ropes and oxen. The holes were filled back with shovels, waiting for new trees to replace the old. It was a repeat of nature's own cycle, life replacing death, the world moving on.

Zech put Frog in charge of the homestead as he and Glenda and Sol set out for Fort Dallas to make good his promise to Tobias to replant the grove. Zech and Glenda rode in the buckboard pulled by two horses, Sol mounted on Tiger. In addition to supplies for the trip, the buckboard contained one steamer trunk loaded with sacks of Spanish doubloons.

From Fort Pierce they headed south on a narrow dirt road paralleling Henry Flagler's railroad, stopping to watch as smoke-belching steam engines labored down the steel rails, causing great flights of birds to flap away in terror. Alligators stalked long-snouted garfish in canals dug by the road builders, and turtles sunning themselves on mudbanks paid no heed to any of it. Zech marveled that anyone could have ever pushed such a ribbon of crushed rock and steel through what once had been jungles of palmetto and Spanish bayonet and swamps where even a horse could not pass.

The trip down the coast took five days and turned into a holiday outing, the first such venture for Zech and Glenda and Sol. Always before there had been cattle to drive and daily chores to do and nothing unusual to see except endless miles of brown prairie and palmetto plains, cypress stands that all looked the same, murky swamps that warned them to turn away. Now they drank in unfamiliar sights along the coastline like revelers, sometimes crossing the tracks and making their way to the beach where they camped on soft sand and cooked sea turtle eggs in the coals of a fire. And then Zech would remember the purpose of the mission and push south at a faster pace.

They finally reached a settlement of shacks west of Palm Beach where the railroad ended. It was in these clapboard houses where servants lived, black mostly but Spanish and white also, people who worked in hotels and dining rooms, cleaned the shops, tended flower gardens and cut grass by day and streamed back to the shacks at night like ants returning to a hill.

When they crossed over to Palm Beach proper it was like entering a make-believe fantasy world. Stores along the main showed gowns from Paris, men's fashions from London, pastries of all shapes and sizes, fine wines and champagne, sausages and cheese from New York. Women walked from store to store beneath dainty parasols, and men wore three-piece vested suits and bowler hats, and some were dressed in knickerbockers with bright-colored socks coming up to their knees. Couples rode down sandy streets in two-seater wicker chairs on wheels.

They turned down another street leading to the beach, both sides lined with stately royal palms. Then they came on it suddenly, the Royal Poinciana Hotel, one of the largest wooden buildings in the world and the largest resort hotel anywhere. The 1,150 guest rooms were made possible by five million feet of lumber, 1,400 kegs of nails, 360,000 shingles, a half-million bricks, 4,000 barrels of lime, and 240,000 gallons of paint. The grounds were aflame with red poinsettia and blue plumbago.

Twelve hundred windows blinked back at him as Zech stared open-mouthed and exclaimed, "Just look at that! I didn't know there were enough trees in all the world to make that many boards! Where you reckon Mister Flagler got it all?"

"I don't know," Glenda responded, "but it's sure something to see."

"Let's stay in it tonight, Pappa!" Sol urged, bouncing up and down in the saddle. "Go on in there and get us a room!"

"Shoot, Sol, we go in there in these wore-out jeans, they'd kick us out faster than a rabbit taking off in front of a wolf. This place is for rich fancy folks, not prairie dogs. They wouldn't even let us eat in the kitchen with the hired help."

"You're probably right," Glenda said. "But let's do go inside and look. We may never come this way again, and it won't hurt anything just to look."

"All right, we'll give 'er a shot," Zech said, getting down and tying the horses.

They crossed the wide veranda and entered two huge oak doors with stained glass panels, coming into a lobby lined with satin-covered chairs and couches. Overhead, a gigantic chandelier with hundreds of French crystal prisms sparkled brightly with the soft glow of electric light bulbs.

"How in the world do they do that, Pappa?" Sol asked, staring upward. "Them's not candles, or coal oil either. How they make it shine just sitting up there?"

"It's electric lights," Zech responded, staring too. "I heard about it in Fort Pierce once. They say it's coming there too someday. A fellow named Ed-sun made it, and he also made a thing that makes music come out of a box. I'll bet there's one of them around here sommers."

"I'd sure like to see it if it is," Sol said, becoming more excited.

"Why don't you go over and at least ask about a room?" Glenda said. "Surely we can afford to stay here for one night, and Sol would really enjoy it."

"I'll do that, but I got an idea it's not going to come out too good."

Glenda and Sol continued touring the lobby as Zech crossed the room to a counter on the far left side. A man in a white suit watched as he approached.

"I'd like a room here for the night. I can pay cash."

"Do you have a reservation?" the man asked.

"Reservation? What's that?"

"Did you write or wire ahead and ask for a room?"

"No, I didn't. We're just passing through, on the way to Fort Dallas. I didn't know this hotel was here till we seen it. And we just want to stay for a night."

"Well, I'm afraid nothing is available," the man said. "There are several boarding houses to the west of here. I suggest you give them a try."

"Thanks anyway," Zech said. "But in case we come back this way from Fort Dallas, how much does it cost to stay the night here? I might could make one of those reservations."

"Rooms start at fifty dollars a night and go up, and suites start at three hundred."

"Oh my goodness!" Zech exclaimed. "It's fifty cents a night at the boarding house in Punta Rassa. It's a good thing you sold out before we got here. A man would be crazy to pay three hundred dollars just to sleep. That's as much as I get for eight or ten cows."

"We're not in the cattle business. And there's no need for you to try here coming back. We're booked solid for the rest of the year. You'll have to look elsewhere."

"I'll do that!"

When he came back across the lobby Sol ran to him and said, "Pappa, you ought to see in that room over yonder! It's an indoor outhouse, and they got stools with lids you can sit on. When you pull a chain it flushes everything away with water. You ought to see it, Pappa! I pulled the chain six times, and it worked ever time!"

"I seen enough in here without something stupid like that. Go and get your mamma and let's leave before they charge us for the water you used."

Glenda came to them and said, "Well, what did they say?"

"You got to have something called a reservation. The man said we ought to try a boarding house."

They went back to the main street and tied the buckboard again, walking sidewalks and gazing into storefronts. One shop sold only birds, colorful macaws and parrots and small canaries. Sol went inside, pointed to a parrot and said, "How much you get for a bird like that?"

"Two hundred dollars," the clerk said, supposing that Sol would not be a customer.

"He's not as pretty as a Carolina parakeet," Sol said, looking in other cages. "But they're all dead now. The freeze killed them."

"Yes, I know. We used to sell them too when we could get them."

"How much is that little yellow bird?"

"Twenty-five dollars each. They're canaries."

"Wow! He's awful little to cost that much. Birds must sell real good here. What do folks do with them?"

"Carry them back up north and keep them as house pets. We sell everything we can get in the store. Are you interested in buying something or just asking questions?"

"Well, maybe I'll buy something," Sol said, his mind racing. "What about those wooden cages? How much are they?"

"Just a cage?"

"No, a bunch of 'em."

"How many would you want?"

"Two dozen."

"I've never sold just cages alone, but for that many I could let you have them for a dollar each."

"Can I pick them up first thing in the morning?"

"I come in the shop at six o'clock. Just knock on the door and I'll let you in."

Sol went back to the sidewalk and ran to catch up with his

mother and father. He said, "Pappa, can I have a couple of coins to spend myself?"

"Sure. I'll give them to you when we get back to the buckboard."

"Can I use the buckboard for a little while first thing in the morning?"

"I suppose so. But why do you want it?"

"I've got a thing to do, and it won't take long. I'll be real careful with it, Pappa. I just want to go back out of town a ways."

"You can do whatever you want tomorrow, but come sunup the next day we've got to push on. We best go on now and find us a place to stay. I don't believe folks here would look kindly if we camped out on the street."

Had it not been for Glenda wanting to stay another day and enjoy browsing through the shops, Zech would have preferred to leave right then and camp in the woods. To him it seemed impossible that such splendor could exist just a few miles from the wilderness. People and animals out there were starving, scratching desperately for survival; yet here there was an abundance of everything. Just the thought of it was repulsive, and he wanted no more of Palm Beach.

Sol ran on ahead to the buckboard, and as Zech and Glenda walked together he said absently, "All this is just the start of it."

"The start of what, Zech?"

"Someday the railroads will haul folks in here thicker than deer flies, and it'll spread elsewhere. I'm glad pappa never saw such as this. It would 'a killed him quicker than the malaria and the cold."

"You're not making sense to me."

"I suppose not. Maybe someday all this will make sense to Sol, but not to me. I've lived too long out yonder to change now. I guess I'm just a dumb cracker, like Pappa."

"Well, it just so happens I like dumb crackers," she said, taking his arm in hers. "What say after we get a place to stay we find a café that serves fried chicken? We haven't had that since Punta Rassa."

"That would be fine. There's bound to be some place here that don't require a reservation just to eat. Fried chicken sounds good to me."

Sol left before breakfast the next morning, and by nine o'clock he still had not returned to the boarding house. Glenda was worried about him, but Zech assured her he was old enough to look out for himself and would return soon.

They left the boarding house and crossed the bridge leading back to the main section of Palm Beach, enjoying the cool breeze that came in from the ocean and the scent of flower gardens that bordered houses.

Zech walked on alone, idly watching carriages pass by and the funny little bicycle carts.

At the next corner he stopped and stared at his own buckboard tied there. Sol was accepting money from an elderly man dressed in knickers, and he continued staring as the man walked away briskly in the direction of the Royal Poinciana, carrying a caged bird in his left hand.

There were six more cages on the buckboard, each containing a small bird with frizzy white fuzz and feathers. Zech walked over rapidly and said, "Sol, what are you doing?"

Sol grinned, and then he said, "I'm selling birds, Pappa, just like the shop down the street."

"Selling baby buzzards?" Zech asked.

"They ain't buzzards," Sol said. "They're kookabens, brought over from Cuba on a schooner. They'll turn green and red when they grow up, and they'll sing just like them little yellow birds in the shop."

Zech stared at the cages again, and then he said, "Son, don't try to fool your daddy. Them's buzzards! I seen a million of 'em in my day."

"All right, Pappa, they're buzzards," Sol admitted. "I done

sold eighteen at twenty-five dollars apiece, and I didn't have to climb but six trees to get 'em. One man was so glad to get his that cheap he gave me an extra ten dollars. I only got six more to sell, Pappa. Please let me finish it."

"My goodness!" Zech exclaimed, shaking his head. "Me an' Pappa thought we'd done something when we sold our first wild cows for fifteen dollars each. What you're doin' seems down-right dishonest to me, but I guess if a man's fool enough to pay three hundred dollars for a hotel room for one night he can afford another twenty-five for a buzzard."

"I'm not making nobody buy 'em, Pappa. They all seem to want one real bad 'cause mine are cheaper than the ones at the bird store."

"Kookabens! What you reckon them folks will do when they get back home and them things turns black and gets so big they flap right off, carrying cage and all?"

"I don't know, Pappa. But I won't be there to find out."

"You sell the rest of them things, that's six hundred dollars for a batch of buzzards. I guess you're going to make out all right, Sol, but I sure wouldn't want to do business with you. Maybe I ought to go out to the woods and shinny up a tree myself. But I best go on back and steer your mamma in another direction. If she sees you on the street sellin' buzzards, she'll most likely have a faintin' spell. You hurry up and get done with it, and don't you do it no more!"

"Thanks, Pappa. It won't take long. Everybody who comes by wants to buy one. I wish I'd got more of them but I only had twenty-four cages."

As Zech turned and walked back up the street a man and a woman stopped at the buckboard, looking curiously at the fuzzy birds. He glanced back as the man picked up a cage and handed it to the woman; then he muttered, "Kookaben birds! What some folks won't buy!"

Zech was at the livery stable at dawn the next morning, hitching up the buckboard to resume the trip. He said to the stable owner, "Is there any special way a man ought to go to get down to Fort Dallas?"

"Yep, sure is. Leave that rig here and take a schooner. That's the best way."

"Well, I don't want to do that. I've got to take my trunk along, and it's too heavy to lug on board a boat and then off again."

"Too heavy for a schooner? What you got in there, gold bars?"

"Nope. Coins."

The man gave Zech a strange look. "You can make it in the rig, but you'll have your work cut out for you. Just follow the only trail going that way. But I still say if I was you I'd take a schooner. How come you want to go to that godforsaken place anyway?"

"Got business there. And thanks for the information."

"Must be going into the skeeter business," the man said as Zech drove off.

As soon as he got back to the boarding house they set forth again, Zech gladly leaving Palm Beach behind. Sol was still happy with his sack of buzzard money safely tucked into his saddlebag.

At first the dirt road was easily passable, running a few miles inland from the ocean. Just before they reached Lake Worth at noon, they passed through an area planted heavily with pineapples, stopping briefly to gather some for their next meal.

They could not pass between the lake and the ocean because someone had cut a canal from the beach into the fresh water lake, turning it to salt; so they skirted the west shore and then turned south again.

Later that afternoon they stopped and made camp in a hardwood hammock and were immediately introduced to mosquitoes that would plague them for the rest of the trip. They came in clouds, swarming over arms and faces. Zech and Sol built two huge fires, throwing on green wood to create as much smoke as possible, but still they came. All of them slept that night with blankets pulled over their heads, suffering the heat in order to keep off the mosquitoes.

From this point south the passable area gradually narrowed to a thin strip separating ocean and palmetto jungle in the east from the vast Pay-Hay-Okee that stretched away endlessly to the west.

The further south they moved, the worse became the trail, and after three more days they came into a jungle of trees and vines, reminding Zech of the custard-apple forest on the western shore of Okeechobee.

They were all beginning to believe there was no Fort Dallas when finally they came into an area planted with oranges, lemons, limes, figs and guavas, mangoes and bananas and avocados–the first sign of humans since leaving Lake Worth.

When they made camp for the night, Sol ate bananas as quickly as he could zip the peels off, unconcerned that he was harvesting someone's fruit. They were so plentiful that a few wouldn't matter, and the evening meal also included bowls of ripe figs and guavas.

At mid-morning the next day they came to the remains of the old fort, finding that someone had changed part of it into a house. Just past this there was a scattering of shacks and a weathered building that served as a post office, land office, and store. Across from this were the schooner docks.

Zech paused and said, "It sure don't look like much. Reminds me of the first time I saw Punta Rassa. Only this place is not even near as big as that."

"I just hope we get what we came after," Glenda said. "I would hate to make a trip all the way down here for nothing. It seems like the end of the world, and I can't for the life of me see why anyone would ever want to live here."

"Me neither," Sol said. "The skeeters is big enough to suck a horse dry."

"There'll be people aplenty when they find out it didn't freeze here," Zech said. "You can count on that. It won't stay like this forever. After we buy the trees, I think I'll spend all the gold that's left on land."

"I don't know what we'd ever do with land here," Glenda said, "but I guess buying it would be better than carrying coins all the way back to the hammock."

They chose an area beneath a thick growth of coconut palms to make camp, and Sol immediately shinnied up the thin trunk of one tree, trying to reach the green nuts.

Glenda shouted up to him, "Come down from there, Sol! You're not a monkey!"

"Sometimes it seems he is," Zech said. "While you're trying to get him back on the ground I'll walk over to the store and ask about the trees."

"Could you buy something there for us to eat? It's just too hot right now to build a fire and cook."

"I'll see what they got," Zech replied, walking off.

The storekeeper was a short fat man in his late forties, wearing a huge straw hat and brown leather sandals with no socks. His thin cotton clothes hung loose over his body and looked more like pajamas than a shirt and pants.

Zech entered and said to him, "Howdy. Name's Zech MacIvey."

"Sam Potter. I seen you come in with that rig. You drive it all the way down here or did the wind blow you in from sommers?"

"Drove it from Palm Beach. And before that, the Kissimmee River."

"You got guts. What can I do for you?"

"I'm interested in buying orange trees."

"Got caught by the freeze, eh? We heard about it. Felt real sorry for you people. How many trees you got in mind?"

"How much they cost?"

"Can let you have cuttins for five cents each. Trees cost a quarter. When the trees are bigger you can make your own cuttins."

"I'm not interested in nothing but trees. Cows eat them cuttins right up. I'll take eight thousand trees for a start."

"How many?"

"Eight thousand to begin with, and as many more as I can get ever month or so. I aim to end up with about ten thousand acres in trees."

"That's a heap. But you sure can't get many trees in that buckboard. Best way is for me to ship 'em up the coast to Fort Pierce by schooner and you pick 'em up there."

"That'd be fine. I'm not too far out from Fort Pierce."

"Eight thousand trees is two thousand dollars. What you got to pay with?"

"Spanish gold doubloons."

"Good enough!" Potter said, smiling. "Can't do better than that. Most folks tries to pay me off with coconuts. That's why I always ask the manner of payment before striking a deal. I ain't seen gold in a coon's age."

"Can you ship me a thousand more ever month till I send word I got enough?"

"No problem."

"How will I pay you?"

"The skipper is a friend of mine. You can pay him when he brings the trees. He docks at Fort Pierce twice a month on a Monday, 'less the weather messes him up. I'll ship 'em so they'll arrive the first Monday ever month and you can meet him there."

"That's real fine. As soon as we eat I'll come back and pay you for the first batch. I might be interested in buying some land too. How much is it?"

"Well, right now the going price is a dollar an acre, but it won't stay that way for long. We're trying to get Flagler to run his railroad on down here, and if he does, the price is sure to go up. It'll go to five dollars an acre, maybe more. Now's a good time to buy."

"I'll think it over and let you know. What you got to eat my wife don't have to cook?"

"Fresh smoked fish, canned beans and tinned beef. You want some fruit, just go out and pick it. Folks here don't care."

"We done that already. I'll take a big batch of smoked fish and a half-dozen cans of beans. I been hankerin' for some beans lately, and my son Sol likes 'em too."

Potter put the items in a sack and said, "You don't owe me nothin'. It's on the house. I ain't traded none for gold in a long time. It's a pleasure dealin' with you."

"Same here, and thanks. I'll see you again in a short while."

The fish was delicious, thick slabs of king mackerel and amber-jack, and Sol capped it off with three cans of beans, followed by Zech with two. All of it was washed down with thick, creamy milk from several coconuts Sol brought down from the tree.

Zech said to Glenda, "I'm only going to have to put out two thousand in cash for the trees, and I'll pay for the others as they come to Fort Pierce. There's over eight thousand in gold in the trunk, so I might as well go on and spend it down here. I'll keep enough for us to get home on and buy land with the rest."

"Whatever you say, Zech. I know there's plenty more gold at the house, and it just takes up room in the buckboard. Maybe land here will be worth something someday."

"It ain't too bad a place except for getting here and the skeeters. But it looks like things sure grow good down here."

"I want to buy some land too," Sol said, listening to the conversation.

"What for?" Zech asked, surprised. "How come you'd want to do that? I'll put everbody's name on the deed and it'll be yours as much as mine."

"I just want to do it myself, Pappa," Sol insisted. "I've got the money I made in Palm Beach."

"What money?" Glenda asked.

"Never mind about it," Zech said to Glenda quickly. "He sold some stuff he gathered in the woods. It's your money, Sol. Just do what you want with it and shut up."

"What kind of stuff?" Glenda then asked.

"Just stuff, Glenda," Zech said. "That's all. It didn't amount to nothin'."

Glenda wasn't satisfied, but she dropped the questioning and said, "While you two are over at the store I'm going to walk to the old fort and look around. I'll meet you back here later."

"Come on, Sol, let's go talk to the man and see what we can do," Zech said.

As they led the buckboard to the store, Sol said, "Thanks, Pappa."

"You're welcome. But next time you better think before you talk in front of your mamma. You'll get yourself in trouble if you don't."

Zech tied the horses and then removed four sacks of coins from the trunk. He and Sol carried them inside and put them on a counter, and Zech said to Potter, "There's more here than I owe for the trees, so just count it later and hold on to the rest. We want to talk now about land."

"You decided what you want to do?" Potter asked.

"Yeah. I want six thousand acres, and Sol wants to buy a little on his own."

"Six thousand acres," Potter repeated. "That's real good, Mister MacIvey. Any special place you want it?"

"I wouldn't know one from the other. You got any suggestions?"

"All the land from here south would be real good if it was cleared. Would make a fine farm. Let's block it out there."

"Suits me. What about you, Sol? You want him to just pick out some for you?"

"What's on that land you can see over yonder across the bay?" Sol asked.

"Well, there's a right nice beach over there if you can push through the mangrove swamps to get to it. Plenty of skeeters too. It ain't fittin' to plant crops on, but if you want some land over there, I can drop the price to fifty cents an acre."

"That's what I want, over yonder on the beach," Sol said. "I've got enough for twelve hundred acres."

"You sure about this?" Potterquestioned. "I don't want you to come back later and think I cheated you."

"It don't look like much from here," Zech said, "but it ought to be worth twenty-four buzzards. Go on and sell it to him if that's what he wants. It's his money, free and clear."

"Ain't no buzzards over there I know of," Potter said, puzzled by the remark. "It's mostly pelicans and gulls."

"Never mind," Zech said. "I don't think Sol's going in the bird business again. When can you have the deeds ready?"

"I'll try to get it done this afternoon. If I don't, sometime tomorrow. And I'll tell you for a fact, Mister MacIvey. You ain't making no mistake. We're putting in for a state charter to make this place Dade County, and when that goes through we're going to name the village Miami."

"Miami? I know a Indian medicine man first name of Miami. He saved my pappa from dying of malaria. But I never asked him what the name means."

"It's Seminole for 'very large.'"

Zech laughed, and then he said, "That's kind of a joke, ain't it? I haven't seen a dozen people since I been here."

"You will if you stay long enough. As I say, you ain't making no mistake. That railroad comes here, your land will be worth at least five bucks an acre and go up from there. Even that land over across the bay might be worth something someday. It's got a right pretty beach if you can find it."

"Can you help us bring in the gold?" Zech asked. "It's kinda heavy."

"My pleasure. And after we get done with it, I want to give you some red snapper for your supper. Friend of mine brings it to me fresh ever day. I'll tell your missus how to cook it like we do down here. It's been soaking in coconut milk all morning, so it ought to be real good come supper time."

That night Glenda cooked a supper as instructed by Potter. He gave them two whole snappers of five pounds each, and she wrapped them in banana leaves and baked them at the edge of the fire. Avocados were cut in half and stuffed with crabmeat provided by Potter, then steamed in an inch of water in the Dutch oven. There was also fresh boiled shrimp, and mangoes so ripe they poured juice when opened.

By the time the meal was finished all of them were stuffed. Zech leaned back against a palm trunk and said, "As far as vittles goes, this place ain't bad at all. Not bad. That supper was real fittin'. A man could sure get plenty to eat here without working so hard at it like we have to do back at the hammock."

"I met a real nice lady this afternoon when I went for a walk," Glenda said. "Name of Julia Tuttle. She lives in the old fort and has fixed it up real nice. She said it's not bad living here once you get used to the isolation, and that's what most folks here want anyway. Flowers grow all year long, and vegetables too. She said there's so many fish in the bay you just scoop out what you want with a net. And they have mail service too. A man walks barefooted all the way down the beach from Palm Beach and brings it here."

"He must have the biggest set of clod-hoppers in the world to walk that far over sand," Zech said. "I'll bet his feet looks like barrel lids."

"She sure told me a lot of things," Glenda said. "She sent Mister Flagler some orange blossoms up to Palm Beach to show him it didn't freeze here, and because of it he might run his railroad down here."

"I don't know why the folks here would want that," Zech said. "This place ever gets like Palm Beach, it's ruined for sure. Why would they want to bring hotels and them wicker bicycles and all that other cruddy stuff down here?"

"That's not what they want at all," Glenda said. "She said they just want folks to come here and build nice little houses and clear the land for planting. It is a real pretty place once you think on it."

"Don't matter what she wants, or the others either. If that engine comes puffin' in here with people packed in like sardines, it's going to mean nothin' but ruination. It'll end up just like Palm Beach. But it sure sounds like that woman done a sellin' job on you. You want to come down here and live?"

"Oh no!" Glenda said quickly. "I wouldn't leave our hammock for anyplace! But maybe someday we could build a little cabin here like the one in Punta Rassa. We could come down by boat from Fort Pierce. It might be fun to come back once in a while and eat the fish and mangoes. And I could visit again with Julia."

"Let's do it!" Sol exclaimed. "Next time we're here I want to see my beach. I want to see what's over there, Pappa."

"We'll think on it," Zech said. "But soon's we get the deeds tomorrow we got to clear on out of here. We still got cows to mark and more holes to dig in the grove. We sure want to be ready when the orange trees get to Fort Pierce. I aim to build Pappa the biggest grove in the whole state."

It was not until noon the next day when Potter handed Zech the deeds, repeating, "You ain't made no mistake, Mister MacIvey."

After promises to return, Zech turned the buckboard north, now much lighter because of an empty trunk.

The first night they camped again at the edge of a lush grove, gorging for the last time on bananas and mangoes, and also tormented by mosquitoes. Then they moved slowly back up the coast.

Zech skirted to the west of Palm Beach, not wanting even the sight of it to come back in his mind. He was also anxious now to reach the lower Kissimmee and that final stretch toward home.

As the horses plodded slowly across the open prairie, bringing back the familiar sights of cypress stands and palmetto and cabbage palms and herds of deer and great flights of birds, Zech was troubled by the things he had seen, contrasting such a place as Palm Beach with the land that was still wilderness, some of it yet untouched by a white man's boots.

There was no doubt in his mind there would be other Palm Beaches, the next most likely at Fort Dallas, but he hoped they would be confined to the coastal beaches and never turn inland, never come even close to his Kissimmee River hammock.

Spring
1896

Zech stood by the empty holding pen, which was located seventeen miles south of the main corral.

Frog rode from the woods and came to him, saying, "I found where they was camped, Mistuh Zech. They's empty bean cans a mile over yonder. Couldn't 'a been more than two days ago."

"A hundred head!" Zech exclaimed, exasperated. "This keeps up we might as well let them drive the herd to Punta Rassa and sell it themselves."

Rustling had become rampant, not only with Zech but with other cattlemen throughout the area. A month earlier Zech and Frog followed the trail of sixteen stolen cows as far south as Fort Pierce. Three miles outside the town they found the hides and heads in a palmetto grove, showing the rustlers had killed the beeves and sold the meat to someone in Fort Pierce. There was no way for them to find out who bought the beef since dressed cows carry no brand. The trail of this herd led to the southwest.

Frog said, "You want to go after them? 'Less they're runnin' them cows full gallop we can catch up with 'em in a few days."

"Wouldn't be no use just you and me doing it. I counted almost a dozen horse tracks. They'd bushwhack us for sure. But I got a idea how to stop it. Let's ride on back north and we'll talk about it later."

That night at supper Zech was strangely quiet, and Glenda suspected something was bothering him more than usual. She knew about the stolen cows and shared his concern, but she had never seen him as angry as he was when he rode in that afternoon.

Zech toyed with his food, and finally he turned to Frog and said, "You been around more places than me, Frog, what with all them trips you've taken after drives and when we don't have much to do. What's the roughest town there is, with the meanest men you can find anywhere?"

"There ain't no doubt about that one," Frog mumbled, his mouth full of roast beef. "It's Arcadia. They's about fifty fights a day there, and as many as four killins 'tween sunup and sundown. Last time I was there some fellows whupped the stew outen me just 'cause they didn't like the cut of my britches. You aim to go there and give it a shot?"

"No. That's not what I've got in mind. Can you hire gun-slingers there?"

"You can go into Arcadia and get anybody you want."

"I want six men to ride south with me. I'll pay five hundred dollars each for the job."

"What on earth are you talking about?" Glenda asked, alarmed by the conversation. "You sound like you're going to start a war somewhere."

"I am. I'm going to settle it once and for all with them rustlers. I know who's doing it, and I know where they're at. If we don't stop it now, we might as well get out of the cattle business and turn the whole prairie over to them."

"I still don't understand," Glenda said. "How could you know these men? You've never seen even one of them."

"Indians told me a good while ago there's a nest of outlaws down south of Punta Rassa, at the edge of the Ten Thousand Islands. I heard it too in Punta Rassa last time we was there, and also in Kissimmee. Other folks has been hit by the same men. It's said that a man named Wirt McGraw is the leader, and everbody is afraid to go after him. Well, I ain't. I don't mind poor folks livin' out in the woods taking a few cows to eat, but that's not what these outlaws is doing. Unless they done passed on by now, some of these men are the same varmints that killed my dogs and Ishmael and caused me and you to lose a baby. I'm going after them, and I should 'a done it before now."

"That's the most foolish thing I've ever heard you say!" Glenda said, even more alarmed. "You'll get yourself killed!"

"Maybe yes, and maybe no," Zech replied calmly. "But I'm tired of wondering if somebody hiding behind a bush is going to blow my head off ever time I ride through the woods. There ain't no law out here to do anything about it, and you know that; so if we don't do something ourselves, nobody will. I know of at least six cattlemen who'll join me, and with six gunslingers, that ought to even the odds. We can ride in real quiet and pop them good before they know what's happening. They think nobody's got the guts to come after 'em. I know there's always going to be rustling, so long as there's men and cows, but if we can put a stop to this bunch it'll be a warning to others. At least it'll make 'em think twice. But as long as we just sit by and do nothing it's an open invitation to any varmint with a horse and a gun. They'll know they can get away with it, and it'll never end. Not ever."

"What you want me to do?" Frog asked, glancing at Glenda.

"I'm not asking anybody here to go with me that don't want to," Zech said. "That's not what you and Lester is being paid for. All I want you to do, Frog, is take the money and hire the men in Arcadia. Then you can come on back here if you want to. I'll pick up the other ranchers and meet your men at the cabin in Punta Rassa. We'll ride south from there."

"You can count me in all the way," Frog said. "I'd purely enjoy bein' a part of this trip. We'll wipe out that buzzard's nest as clean as a whistle."

"What about you, Lester?" Zech then asked.

"Well, I don't know, Mistuh Zech. I don't want you to think I got no guts, an' I'm willin' to do whatever you say, but I'm sure not much good with a gun. All I ever done is punch cows."

"Then you won't go, and there's no hard feeling at all. You can stay here with Glenda and Sol."

"I want to go too, Pappa!" Sol said. "I can shoot a rifle good as anyone!"

"No way!" Zech said. "You'll stay behind with your mamma. And that's that!"

"I'll not stay here either!" Glenda snapped. "Not while you're way off down there getting yourself shot at! Sol and I'll go with you to Punta Rassa and stay in the cabin. That way we'll know real soon if you'll ride back with us or if we bring you back in a box. I'll not sit here all that time wondering!"

"You can do that if you want," Zech said, "but nobody's coming back in a box. I'm not a fool. We'll be real careful and do this thing right. Frog, you go to Arcadia and come on to Punta Rassa soon as you can. I'll round up the other cattlemen and go straight there. Lester, you stay here and look after the place. We'll leave at sunup."

"I still think this is stupid!" Glenda said. "But I can see there's no way to talk you out of it."

"It's a thing that's got to be done, either now or later," Zech replied. "There's no way out of it, so what's the use of putting it off any longer."

*F*rog arrived in Punta Rassa one day later than Zech. After taking one brief look at the group Frog was leading, Glenda went into the cabin and shut the door.

Each man was over six feet tall, slim as a rail, filthy and bearded, wearing a black felt hat and clothes that hadn't been washed for a year. They were all hungry looking, and the only thing separating them from the dead was the fact they were breathing. None of them returned Zech's greeting as they dismounted in front of him. They simply walked off to a nearby tree and squatted.

Zech said in hushed tones, "Frog, that's the meanest looking bunch I ever seen."

"That's what you wanted, ain't it?"

"I guess so. But the smell. We'll have ever buzzard on the west coast following us."

"Just watch where you ride," Frog said. "If the wind comes from the south while we're headed down that way, go in front of them. If it's from the north, ride behind. That way it ain't so bad. I found that out comin' here. But if there ain't no wind, Lord help us. We're in a heap of trouble."

"Maybe we can stand it for a couple of days," Zech said.

"I done things a little different from what you wanted, Mistuh Zech. I only gave 'em two hundred each to begin with, and promised the rest when the job is done. That way they won't hightail it off before we even get there."

"That's a good idea. I wouldn't trust that bunch with a bucket of slop. They'd probably be in the hog business and make off with it."

"Where's your men?" Frog asked.

"At the boarding house. I got seven ranchers from Kissimmee. Word spread here what we're going to do, and when they found out about the men you're bringing, they all seemed to get courage they ain't never had. Six more cowmen wants to join up. That'll make twenty-one of us altogether. I'll go on down there now and bring the rest back here."

Zech returned in a half hour leading the troop. He went into the cabin briefly to say good-bye to Glenda.

"Please be careful, Zech," she pleaded. "I feel better now with so many of you, but don't take foolish chances."

"We won't. I promise you. And we ought to be back here day after tomorrow. It's only about sixty miles down there, so we'll probably hit them first thing in the morning."

The group rode away briskly, cantering the horses, looking like a small army, however ragtag.

They had been gone no more than ten minutes when Glenda heard a horse come galloping past the front of the cabin. She rushed outside, seeing Sol jump a split-rail fence and head toward the holding pens where the men disappeared.

She shouted frantically, "Sol! Sol MacIvey! Come back here! You come back here this instant!"

He merely waved back at her, then went past the pens and turned south.

She leaned against the outside cabin wall, staring after him, and then she said, "You men! MacIveys! I hope Zech has the sense to send you back!"

The men rode steadily all afternoon, staring straight ahead, each knowing the danger they faced. When night came they continued on for an hour; then they stopped and made a fireless camp beneath a grove of oaks, eating cold beans from cans.

Frog's recruits still had not spoken one word to anyone. At dawn they ate more beans and set out again, but this time they rode slowly. Zech finally signaled everyone to stop, and then he said, "We must be awful close now. Me and Frog'll ride out a ways and see what's ahead. Everybody else wait here till we get back."

They moved through a thick hardwood hammock that ended at an open field; then they dismounted and crept forward, hiding behind a clump of cocoplum bushes. Sugar cane in the field had come up to a height of one foot. Across from the field there were several cabins, a barn, and a corral filled with cattle. Off to the right a dock ran out into a bay heavily dotted with small mangrove islands.

A fire blazed under what looked at a distance to be a whiskey still, and over another fire, close by one of the cabins, a whole steer was roasting on a spit. Zech counted twenty-three men moving about, one of them hobbling on a wooden leg.

They eased back to the horses and returned to the waiting men. Zech said, "Best as I could tell, there ain't no more of them than there are of us. And they is so sure of themselves they don't even have a guard out. We'll catch 'em by surprise for sure. The whole area around the camping area is open land, so we'll divide into groups and ride in from three sides. In the west there's water. Frog, you take your men around to the south. Six of you stay here with me, and the rest can come in from the east. Watch the line of woods over this way, and when you see me start across the cane field, ride in and we'll have the whole bunch right in the middle."

As the men broke into groups Zech said, "Good luck, fellows. We'll give you about fifteen minutes to get in place."

Zech led his group of silent men to the edge of the cane field. One of the men plopped a huge plug of tobacco into his mouth, chewed nervously, and spat a brown stream onto the ground.

A lump came into Zech's throat as he stared across the field, watching one man turn the steer as flames licked the meat. He wondered who these men were, where they came from, why they were here and what drove them to do what they were doing; he knew that soon now someone would die, maybe them and maybe himself. Is it really worth all this, he asked himself, all this approaching death because of cows? But he knew it was more than cows that brought him here, remembering the dogs and the horses and the bullet in Bonzo and the bushwhacking and the firefight and the murder of an unborn baby and the absolute need to take these men's lives from them in order to stop it. But why had they started it in the first place? This he couldn't answer, knowing only the fact that some men would rather take than share and would indeed as soon kill another man as a snake.

He was so deep in thought the man next to him had to shake his arm and say, "Ain't it time to go now?"

"Yes. It's time. Everybody ought to be in place. Lord help us . . . and watch over us. . . . Let's go!"

The horses bolted forward, and they were halfway across the field when other groups rushed from woods in the east and south.

They were within one hundred yards of the compound before they were noticed. Then men scrambled frantically into cabins and popped out again, firing rifles. Zech aimed the Winchester as best he could on the bouncing horse, pulling off three shots, then seeing the man at the spit topple forward into the fire and scream wildly as he rolled across the ground.

The three groups had the surprised men. They could hide themselves from north riders, but this exposed them to those coming from the east and south. Before the three groups came together in the middle of the compound, nine men lay dead, three more wounded and crawling in the dirt like dogs.

Frog saw one man jump from behind a woodpile and aim a rifle at him. He dodged sideways as a tiny speck of fire came from the gun barrel; then he felt a sharp pain in his left shoulder, knowing he was hit. He said, "Aw no! . . . you outlaws done it now!" He charged forward, pumping six bullets into the man, four of them hitting him after he lay dead on the ground.

It ended as quickly as it began, men throwing down rifles and holding their arms upward, horses now running around them in circles. Zech brought his horse to a halt in front of the captives and said, "Which one of you varmints is Wirt McGraw?"

The man with the wooden leg hobbled forward. He was in his late sixties, bald and bearded. He said gruffly, "I am, if it's any of your business! And who be you?"

"Zech MacIvey."

"MacIvey, eh. I'll remember the name. When you fools get done with whatever you're here for, I'll take care of you, MacIvey. You can count on it."

"Only thing you can count on is dying!" Zech shot back harshly. "We're goin' to hang the whole lot of you!"

"For what?" McGraw asked. "You can't prove we done nothin' to nobody!"

"We'll see about that. A couple of you men go look in the barn and then see what brands them cows has. Then we'll talk more about why you're going to do a rope dance."

None of them noticed the black marshtackie as it came across the canefield and stopped at the edge of the clearing. The rifle blast caught them by surprise, but before they could turn and see where it came from, a man staggered from the corner of a cabin. He staggered four steps forward and fell, firing the rifle as he went down, the bullet striking Zech's right foot like a hammer, knocking him out of the saddle.

Zech jumped up quickly and looked behind him, seeing Sol's horse trot forward, the Winchester smoking. Sol said, "I had to shoot him, Pappa! He was drawed down on you! I had to do it!"

"What are you doing here?" Zech demanded. "I told you to stay in Punta Rassa with your mamma!"

"I wanted to come, Pappa! I wanted to be here with you!"

"Well, what's did is did," Zech said, his voice calmer. "And I guess it's a good thing you did sneak along. If you hadn't, that varmint would 'a blowed my head off 'stead of my foot. I thank you for that, Sol."

Zech limped to his horse as one man rode into the circle and said, "They's four men chained in that barn, and them cows has got ever brand on 'em you can think of, including MacIvey."

"That's it!" Zech said. "Somebody take the chains off them men and set 'em free, and the rest of you herd these varmints to the nearest tree and string 'em up. Then we'll set fire to this whole stinkin' place and burn all of it to the ground."

McGraw spoke up, "You fellows wouldn't do something like that to a old army buddy, would you? I lost my leg fightin' for the Rebs in the war."

"That ain't what they say in Punta Rassa," Zech said. "Word is you were a deserter and plundered ever homestead you could find without a man there to protect it. And you been at it ever since. Backshootin' included. You can take what's coming to you now like a man, or you can whine like a baby, whichever you choose. It's up to you."

"Blast you!" McGraw bellowed. "Blast all of you! You'd 'a never took us hadn't you snuck in here like wolves! Go on and do it and be done with it!"

"We will!" Zech said. "And you'll be the first! I'd put the rope on you myself if I could walk!"

As the men started herding the captives away, Frog said, "I need a little help, Mistuh Zech. I got a hole in my shoulder."

"And I got a foot that pure hurts like hell," Zech said. "Sol, get down off there and see to Frog. Then help me tie a cloth to my leg to stop the bleeding. Then we better hightail it back to Punta Rassa. They got a doctor there now."

Sol tore up his shirt and made a bandage for Frog's wound. Then he bound Zech's foot and leg. Fires leaped up all around them as they mounted the horses, and at the edge of the east woods, men dangled from the limbs of an oak.

One of the men from Arcadia rode up and spoke for the first time, "We'll take the rest of our money now. Everybody's dead. Anything else you want us to do?"

Frog handed him a sack of gold as Zech responded, "Naw, that's it. We done what we came for. You can leave anytime you want."

"Thanks," the man said, before he galloped away.

"That bunch will all probably kill each other before it's over," Frog said. "I sure wouldn't want to be the one totin' the sack of money."

"Me either," Zech said. "But right now let's make these horses burn dust. My foot feels like ever bone in it is broke."

*Z*ech lay on a cot as the doctor examined his foot. Frog was already bandaged, and Glenda hovered over Zech as the doctor shook his head and said, "I've never seen one like this before. That bullet is buried in bone, with just a tip showing. There's no way I can get it out. I just don't have the tools to do it. Only thing I can do, if you say so, is take off the foot part way up your leg."

"No!" Zech roared. "You ain't goin' to do no such thing! Where's a doctor who can do what needs to be did?"

"Not anywhere around here. Maybe in Jacksonville, and you might have to go all the way to Atlanta to find one. It's going to take a bone specialist with the proper know-how and tools. But you better do something. That bullet stays in there, you'll never walk on that foot again. And you'll probably get lead poisoning."

Zech yelled as the doctor poured whiskey into the open wound. Then he said, "There ain't no way I can stand this much longer. I'd never make it to Jacksonville, much less Atlanta."

"You've got to try, Zech!" Glenda pleaded. "We've got to do something!"

For a moment Zech dropped into deep thought, and then he said, "I know what I'll do. I'll go to the same doctor what saved Pappa. The Seminole medicine man."

"What?" the doctor said. "A medicine man? What's he going to do, dance around in a circle shaking rattles? You best either let me take the foot off or head straight for Jacksonville or Atlanta. Medicine man!"

Zech ignored the doctor as he said, "Sol can ride down there with me, and Glenda, you stay here and tend to Frog till he can ride. Me and Sol'll come straight on back to the hammock from the Indian village."

"Your friend ought to be able to ride in a buckboard in four or five days," the doctor said. "His bullet went clear through but it busted some ribs. He'll have to be careful for a good while."

"Don't worry 'bout us, Mistuh Zech," Frog said. "We'll be fine. Soon's I can move about, me and Miz Glenda'll go on back to the place. We'll see you there."

"Zech, are you sure this is what you want to do?" Glenda asked, deeply concerned. "If the doctor here can't help you, what can a medicine man do?"

"He saved Pappa. That's for sure. And he'll do the same for

me. I sure ain't goin' to hobble around the rest of my life on a wooden stump. I'd look just like that guy we hung down there in the woods. Sol, get the horses ready. We need to get on with it."

"Yessir, Pappa," Sol responded. "I'll give 'em a good feedin' and some water. It won't take but a few minutes."

As Sol went out Zech said to Glenda, "Don't get on him no more for what he done. If he hadn't followed us I'd be dead for sure. He saved me, Glenda. So just don't say nothing more to him."

"I won't. But he sure gave me a fright shucking out of here the way he did."

The doctor picked up his bag and said, "I've done all I can, so I'll leave now. I think you're doing a foolish thing, but it's your foot and your life. You better pray that thing don't get infected. If it does, you're in bad trouble. Medicine man! Good Lord!"

As the doctor left, Zech said, "Glenda, go on out there and hurry Sol up. I don't think I can stand this but just long enough to ride from here to the village. It's a good thing I know the way now."

There were times when Zech didn't know who he was or where he was, the pain shooting up his leg like boiling fire, but he rode on, galloping and then walking the horses to rest them. At dawn they passed by the Okeechobee trading post, and in another two hours they came into the village.

Zech slumped forward in the saddle as Keith Tiger came to him first and said, "Zech?. . . Zech MacIvey?. . . What is the trouble? You seem to be in much pain."

"My foot . . ." Zech muttered. "Bullet . . . the medicine man. . . ."

Toby Cypress then came scrambling from a chickee and said, "Father! It is you! What is the matter?"

"He's been shot," Tiger said. "Help him to the chickee while I get the medicine man. Quickly!"

Sol's eyes widened as he watched the strange boy help Zech from the horse and carry him gently to a cypress table, the words ringing in his ears, "Father . . . it is you." Then he jumped from the horse and helped place Zech back down on the rough planks.

The medicine man was now as old and stooped as Keith Tiger, and he seemed to float as he came across the clearing. He took the foot in his hand and stared at it; then he drew a long hunting knife from his belt and pushed the blade into a fire.

Toby's grandfather and three older men came to the table and held Zech down as Miami Billie said, "This will hurt you, but it will be over soon. Put this piece of hickory in your mouth and bite down on it."

Zech bit the stick viciously as the medicine man leaned down to the wound, his mouth groping, teeth grinding until they took a firm grip on the tip of the bullet; then the knife was inserted into the bone and shaken back and forth, loosening the lead, teeth locking on again as the old man sucked and grunted. Slowly but surely the bullet moved outward, Zech feeling like he would pass out from pain; then suddenly it popped free and Miami Billie stood straight, his face blood-covered, the bullet firmly gripped in his teeth. He spat it out and said, "I will make the poultice now. You may limp, my son, but you will walk."

Those were the last words Zech heard before he fainted, ". . . you will walk."

*W*hen Zech looked up an hour later, Sol and Toby were standing by the table, Sol's eyes both puzzled and hostile as he glared at Toby and then looked to his father. Zech knew why, and he said to Sol, "You heard what Toby said, didn't you?"

"I heard him call you 'father'. What does this mean, Pappa? Do Indians call everbody that?"

"No, they don't. No more than you. Toby is my son, Sol, and your half-brother. His mamma was Tawanda, and she's dead now. I promised her that you and Glenda would never know about this, but what's done now can't be helped. You got to promise me you'll never tell your mamma, Sol. You got to do it. Promise me now!"

"All right, Pappa, I promise. I won't ever tell."

"And I know what you're thinking," Zech said, troubled. "I can see it in your eyes. It wasn't no bad thing, Sol. I knew Tawanda before I married your mamma. Tawanda was a good woman, a real fine person. Do you understand what I'm saying?"

"I'm trying to, Pappa," Sol said, tears forming in his eyes. "Honest I am. But I never knew I had a Indian brother. It'll take some getting used to."

"I'm going to be flat on my back for a few days," Zech said, looking down at what appeared to be a mudpack encasing his foot and leg. "And I don't want you two standing here gawking at me all the time. Go off and do something together. Hunt or fish or ride horses. Get to know each other while you got the chance. You might find out you like each other."

"I can show you Pay-Hay-Okee, the River of Grass, if you would like to see it," Toby said hesitantly, watching Sol's reaction.

The ice suddenly broke. Sol smiled and said, "I'd like that. And I'll bet my marshtackie can outrun yours."

"We'll see," Toby responded as they both scrambled for the horses.

Zech smiled too as he watched them gallop away. He said, "I wish I could go with you. I'd like to see it again myself."

Toby's grandfather came to the chickee and said, "It's good those two have gone away together. I was afraid they would hate each other."

"I was too. Maybe boys can accept things grown folks can't. They might end up friends."

"That is the way it should be. But tell me now. How did you come to have that bullet in you?"

"We wiped out that pack of varmints in the Ten Thousand Islands and one of 'em put it there. They're all dead, so you don't have to worry about them no more. You can tell your people to go there now whenever they like and they won't find trouble."

"I will do this gladly. It took great courage for you to go against those men. Nobody else would."

"It wasn't no big deal at all. We took 'em by surprise and ended it real quick." Zech became silent for a moment, and then he said, "I been thinking of something ever since you came to my place to pay respects to Pappa and told me about Tawanda. You'll have to help me with it."

"What is that?"

"I'm goin' to give money to the man at the Okeechobee trading post so he can hire a stonecutter to make a marker for Tawanda's grave. I'll draw a map, and he can bring it down here in a ox cart. You'll have to show him where to put it."

"Tawanda is resting in the Seminole way, in a casket on top of the ground."

"Then you'll have to bury it. I want you to do this for me. I want her buried like my pappa and mamma. That's the way I want it to be."

"If that is your wish I will do it. I will see to the grave this afternoon, and then watch for the stone to arrive."

"It'll probably be a good while before it gets here, but I sure thank you for letting me do this. It will give me peace of mind knowing it's done."

Zech suddenly felt overwhelmed with tiredness. He said, "I hope them boys has a good time together. Maybe they. . . ." Before he finished, he fell into a deep sleep.

Zech stayed in the village for six more days, the medicine man and two women tending him constantly, changing the poultice and giving him a strong drink made from herbs. The swelling went down rapidly, and on the fourth day he hobbled around with the aid of a hickory cane.

Sol and Toby spent all of each day together, racing the horses and fishing in creeks and ponds. One day they killed a deer and cooked it themselves, feasting with Zech on venison steaks and swamp cabbage prepared by Toby's grandmother.

At daybreak on the seventh day, the medicine man bound Zech's wound for the final time, warning him to be careful on the return trip and rest often. Sol and Toby said warm good-byes, promising to see each other again someday. Then Zech and Sol mounted and rode away slowly, stopping at the edge of the woods and raising their arms in a final salute.

March

1898

"Mistuh Zech, how we gone ever put a mark on that big bull?" Frog asked, looking inside the pen.

"It'll take some doing," Zech replied, scratching his head doubtfully. "It's for sure he's not going to stand there and let us poke him with a hot iron. What we need is ole Skillit to put him on his back."

Inside the pen was a Brahma bull, its huge hump quivering with fury, fifteen hundred pounds of anger wanting to get at the men who put him there. Zech had bought him the previous week from a Texan who brought six of them into Kissimmee by rail and sold them for five hundred dollars each. But he hadn't warned the buyers that these were wild range bulls. The bull was delivered to Zech's corral that morning in an iron cage mounted on wagon wheels, drawn by three oxen.

"He's ugly," Glenda said as she sat on her horse by the fence. "Mean ugly. I don't see what you want with such a creature."

"He ain't pretty, I'll admit," Zech said, "but they say he gets by on less grass than any critter and can stand the heat and ticks better. It's the coming thing, Glenda, and all the cowmen are turning to Brahmas. Besides that, when one of them things is dressed out for beef he's going to look like any other skinned cow. Folks don't buy meat for its looks. And you won't ever see a yellowhammer that big. Beeves his size bring twice as much money. It's like having two grown steers on four legs 'stead of eight."

"Just the same, I think he's disgusting. That hump makes him look like he's deformed."

"You want me and Lester to go in there and see can we get a rope on him?" Frog asked.

"Let's just cool him down a bit first," Zech responded. "Maybe by tomorrow he won't be so cantankerous. We'll let him simmer awhile and try him in the morning."

"I don't think he likes it here, Pappa," Sol said. "I bet if you opened the gate and turned him loose he'd be in Punta Rassa before sundown."

"Maybe so, but I'm not going to find out.

The bull wheeled around constantly, nostrils flaring angrily as he snorted, pawing his front hooves. Saliva streamed from his mouth as he charged forward, shaking his head up and down, then ramming the fence with his horns and backing away.

Frog watched fearfully as the bull rammed the fence again and again, and then he said, "Mistuh Zech, it might take a cypress pole right betwixt his eyes to settle his nerves. You let me bash him two, three times, he'd stop carryin' on so."

"If we had some dogs we could do it," Zech said, limping to his horse. "Else he'd get his hind legs and his nose ripped out. Just let him be for now and we'll try again tomorrow. And Sol, don't you be teasin' him. You'll just make him madder."

"I won't, Pappa. But if I could get on his back I'd break him."

Zech and Glenda rode off together, and when they were past hearing range Glenda said, "Frog's too old to fool with such things as that bull."

"I know," Zech replied. "I worry about him a lot. I've told him a hundred times he can feed the horses and tend the garden but he won't have none of it. An old cracker like him'll keep doin' what he's doin' till he drops dead in the saddle. There's

120

no way to stop him, and I'm sure not going to run him off the place after all the years he's been here with us. If Pappa was alive he'd be the same way. You'd never get Pappa to sit in a rockin' chair and take it easy. He'd be out there doin' something."

"I suppose. But I'd feel better if Frog would slow down. It's time he rested some. And you don't have any business either trying to brand cows with that bad leg. You couldn't get out of the way quickly if you had to. It's downright dangerous."

"I can still move fast enough to look out for myself," Zech said. "I guess I'm lucky to walk at all, but no cow's going to catch me flat-footed. So you best forget that."

They crossed through the hammock and came to the open area of the grove. Zech had gradually increased it to eight thousand acres, just short of his ten-thousand-acre goal; and now the deep green trees marched over the land like rows of silent soldiers. Fruit was no longer carted to Fort Pierce and put on slow boats, but taken to a nearby railhead and shipped rapidly to northern markets. Zech had long since admitted the truth of Tobias' prediction that oranges would become like gold growing on trees. The acreage was now so big it was necessary for him to hire pickers from Kissimmee and Fort Pierce to come in during the season and harvest the crop.

Zech stopped beside one of the trees and examined the acorn-size fruit. "These trees are a lot better than the ones killed by the freeze. We're going to have oranges running out our ears come fall. I wish Pappa could see how well they're doing. He'd be right proud."

"I'm sure he would," Glenda agreed. They moved on silently for a moment, and then she said, "The mangoes should be ripe at Fort Dallas now. I wish we could go back down there. Maybe this time we could build our little cabin."

"We'll go soon as the branding's done. The railroad has been run to Miami now, so we can ride the train all the way. One time before I die I'd like to ride one of them smoke-belchin' devils. Just once, and that'd be enough."

They continued on through the grove, enjoying being alone together, a thing that was impossible back in the hammock where cooking and washing and tending the men's needs took all of Glenda's time. She said, "Zech, why don't we go away together this summer and take a trip. Just the two of us. We've never done anything like that, and it's about time we did something just for pleasure. We've got the money to go anywhere we want to go. We could ride the train up north. Wouldn't you like to see places like Washington and New York and Boston just once? They seem so foreign to us here, they could as well be in Europe. "

"I've never given it any thought, but we could go there if you'd like to. Sol could look after things while we're gone. Fact is, he could take over this place now and run it by himself."

"That's another thing I've been thinking on," Glenda said. "Sol will be fifteen next week, and I've taught him everything I can. He can read and write and work figures as good as anyone, but there's more to learning than that. Maybe we should send him off for more schooling. There's a college now in DeLand."

"Send Sol off to college?" Zech questioned, amused by the thought of it. "How'd we do that? Hog tie him and drag him there? If he ever got to one he'd probably get kicked out for riding his horse into the classroom."

"Be serious, Zech!" Glenda scolded. "It's something to consider. Someday he'll need to know more than riding horses and herding cows and what little I've taught him. You've said yourself Florida is changing."

"It's doing that for sure, and I wouldn't want Sol to be any part of it. I'd hate to even think of him living someday in a place like Palm Beach. Out here is where he belongs, just like you and me and Pappa and Mamma."

"At least think about it," she concluded. "We could do without him here this fall. He could go for a while just to see if he likes it."

"I'll think on it, and if that's what Sol wants to do I won't stand in his way. But it's up to him, Glenda. It's his choice, and I don't think he'll want to do it. He's where he wants to be."

"Maybe so," Glenda sighed, "but there are other things in life besides horses and cows."

Zech shouted, "Sol, stay out of there and let us handle it! And Glenda, keep your horse well away from the fence. If that critter comes bustin' out of the pen, stay out of his way."

The bull had not settled down as Zech hoped, and now he dashed from one side of the pen to another, his eyes wild and his mouth foaming with rage.

Frog said to Zech, "Me and Lester'll go in there and try to get him on the ground. If we do, we can tie his feet and we'll have him for sure. I'd like to be the one to stick a hot iron to him."

"Be careful," Zech cautioned. "If we can't get a mark on him we'll just turn him loose without one. I don't think nobody can catch him and steal him. That Texan must of had some kind of fun catching him and putting him in a boxcar."

"If he did it, we can," Frog said. "I ain't never seen a bull yet that couldn't be throwed one way or another. But I'd sure like to see ole Skillit standin' here now. He'd have that thing down in nothin' flat."

Frog and Lester eased through the gate, and the bull turned to them immediately, pawing his feet and snorting. Frog said, "Move over to the right real slow and draw his attention. If he comes at you, dodge out of the way and I'll put a rope on him."

The bull watched both men for a moment more; then he was attracted to the movement. He snorted again and charged directly at Lester. Frog shouted, "Get outen the way, Lester! Hurry!"

Lester hit the split-rail fence scrambling. He went up the side like a frightened lizard and rolled over the top just as horns crashed into wood. Frog threw the rope, and the noose dropped down over the neck and became tight. Then the bull wheeled and charged away, dragging the struggling Frog in the dirt.

Zech shouted, "Turn loose, Frog! Let go and get out of there!"

Frog didn't let go. He made one circle of the pen behind the flying bull and jumped to his feet when the movement stopped. It took less than two seconds for the bull to charge again, surprising Frog by its quickness, coming at him full bore with no chance to jump aside. One horn smashed through his rib cage and sent him hurling eight feet backward.

Zech opened the gate and ran for the rope, his bad leg tripping him up and sending him sprawling beside Frog, knocking the breath from him. He glanced up as the bull rushed past him and out the gate; then he watched helplessly as it wheeled about and charged the horse, hearing the thud as horns met flesh, then seeing the horse and Glenda topple to the ground.

Zech scrambled to his feet and watched horrified as the horns rammed into Glenda, going into her stomach, staying there. He heard her scream, "Zech! . . . Zech! . . . Help me! . . ."

The bull raised its head upward, lifting her into the air as she screamed again, "Oh! . . . Zech! . . ."

The first bullet caused the bull to stagger, and the second brought it down. As it hit the ground Glenda came loose and tumbled away. Zech ran from the pen as fast as he could, snatching the smoking rifle away from Sol, firing into the dead animal again and again until the chamber was empty, then falling down beside Glenda.

She tried to speak, "Zech . . . Zech. . . ." It turned to a gurgle, and then silence came as her head rolled to the side.

"Oh no . . ." Zech moaned. "Oh no . . . Glenda . . . ."

He fell across the body, unaware as Lester shook his shoulder, saying, "Mistuh Zech! Mistuh Zech! Frog's hurt real bad! What you want me to do?"

He finally looked up and said, "Go and get the buckboard. Hurry! And bring blankets from the house."

Sol staggered forward and said, "Is she dead, Pappa? Is Mamma dead?"

"She's gone from us, Sol. Get on your horse and go to the house as fast as you can. Fetch back the shotgun and a sack of shells."

Sol looked at his father, puzzled by such an order at such a time; then he jumped on his horse and galloped away.

Zech was still holding Glenda in his arms when Sol and Lester returned. His eyes were glazed with anger as he got up and took the shotgun from Sol. He inserted shells and fired pointblank into the bull, doing it again and again until the carcass was cut in half. Then he put the shotgun into the buckboard and went inside the pen to Frog.

Frog was lying still, his eyes hazed but seeing, and when Zech dropped down beside him he said, "Ain't this awful, Mistuh Zech. All the things I've done and got by with, to be did in now by a bull."

"Don't talk," Zech said, pulling Frog's shirt away, seeing a six-inch hole where Frog's side had been. "We'll get you to the house as quick as we can. Then I'll send for a doctor in Kissimmee."

"I'm old enough to know better than that," Frog said weakly. "There's no need for a doctor. Did that critter hurt Miz Glenda when he went for her horse?"

"Yes, Frog, he did. He hurt her real bad."

"Lordy me . . . I'm sorry to hear that, Mistuh Zech. I wish I could 'a kept him here in the pen, but there wadden no way. He was just too strong to handle."

Zech and Lester lifted Frog up gently and carried him to the buckboard. Then Zech picked up Glenda and placed her beside him. He said to Sol, "Leave that varmint right there where he's lying till the buzzards pick him clean. When there ain't nothin' left but bones, I want you to throw 'em in the river. I don't want to ever see nothin' more of him again."

Sol nodded in agreement as Zech climbed onto the buckboard and drove away.

When they reached the hammock Zech and Lester put Frog on his bunk; then Zech carried Glenda into the house alone. He came back out and said to Lester, "Go down to the barn and start a coffin. I just can't bring myself to do it, Lester. You'll have to. And while you're at it, you might as well make two."

"I know, Mistuh Zech. Frog's not goin' to last long. I doubt he'll be here at nightfall. I gave him a big shot of rum to ease the pain, and I'll go back in an hour and give him some more. And don't worry about the coffins. I'll take care of it."

Zech sat on the stoop, his face buried in his hands, remembering, thinking of things done and not done. He also remembered the day of Emma's death when Tobias urged him to do things for Glenda before it was too late.

He was unaware of Sol sitting beside him until he heard the sobbing. He looked up and said, "Sol, don't ever get yourself tied up with a woman. It's like owning dogs. You get to liking them, and it hurts powerful when they go away. And they all go away. If you get to lovin' a woman too much, it'll bring pain and sorrow when she leaves you. It's done hurt me twice, and the pain of it is pure awful. It'll never go away. Don't let it happen to you."

"I don't understand, Pappa," Sol said, wiping away the tears. "Wasn't you glad to live with Mamma?"

"That's just it, son. I liked it too much. And now that it's all done, I'm not sure the joy of it can overcome the pain and sorrow."

"I still don't understand," Sol said.

"I hope you don't ever have the feel of it and have to understand. Maybe it won't come to you like it has to me. And besides that, I know I'm not makin' sense. I didn't expect nothin' like this to happen, Sol. I don't know what I'm going to do without your mamma. I don't rightly know if I can make it or not, or even if I want to try."

"We'll be fine, Pappa," Sol said, putting his arm around Zech's shoulder. "Mamma would want us to try. She wouldn't give up on nothing, and you know that. I'll learn to cook and wash and do all the things she did for us. We'll make out somehow, Pappa."

Zech knew he would have to carry on for Sol's sake, whether he wanted to or not. "But the stuff you're talking about we can't do and run this place too. We'll need a man to replace Frog and a woman to do the rest of it. I'll go first to Fort Drum and tell Glenda's folks about this. Then I'll go to Fort Pierce and see if I can hire somebody with a wife to come live with us. If I can't get somebody there I'll try Kissimmee. But we can talk about this later. Right now I need to look in on Frog."

Just after dark, Frog opened his eyes, seeing Zech sitting beside the bunk. He smiled, and then he said, "Mistuh Zech, I want to ask a favor of you."

"Sure, Frog. Anything you say."

"I come here to help on one cattle drive, the first one your Pappa made to Punta Rassa, and I been here ever since. This hammock's the only home I've had since before the war. I'd like to be buried right alongside Mistuh Tobias and Miz Emma. Don't put me way off in the woods by myself, Mistuh Zech. Please don't do it."

"You'll rest right next to Mamma and Pappa, but I would have done that even if you hadn't asked."

"That's not all of it, Mistuh Zech. I got a good bit of gold over yonder in my locker, and I want you to take it and get me a headstone, like the ones over the other graves. I been here so long now I feel like part of the family, and I'd like the stone to say Frog MacIvey. When ole Skillit dies his is goin' to say Skillit MacIvey, and that's what I want too. Would it be too much of a shame to you if you did this for me?"

Zech reached down and touched the gnarled hand. "It wouldn't be a shame at all, Frog. You're as much family as anybody, and I'll be right proud to get the stone just the way you

127

want it. Mamma and Pappa will like it too, and so will Glenda."

"I thank you, Mistuh Zech," Frog said, smiling again. "I'll tell Mistuh Tobias you done a good job here after he was gone, and about all them trees you planted. He'll be right pleased. . . ."

He drifted away again, and fifteen minutes later he was dead.

It took Zech and Lester and Sol two hours after daybreak to dig the holes, and then the coffins were brought to the gravesite one by one and lowered into the ground.

The three of them stood there silently as birds chattered above them, Zech's eyes now dry because all the tears had flooded out of him the night before. A red fox suddenly popped out of a bush, stared at them for a moment, and then scurried away.

Zech finally said, "Lord . . . I'm not going to say much about this, because if I do, I'm not sure I can stand it. It seems a man is born into life just to suffer and bear grief, and I done suffered enough of it. I want You to forgive me for buyin' that bull, 'cause all I done it for was to make money, and I'll never do nothin' like that again. So help me, Lord, I promise it, but it's too late now to help Glenda and Frog. They suffered because of what I done. Lord . . . bless Glenda. She was as fine a woman as You ever made, and I loved her truly. And bless old Frog too. He done the best he could, Lord . . . the best he could. Make them a home with Mamma and Pappa . . . and see to it they're happy now. . . . Amen."

Zech then turned to Sol, "I'm going to go now, son, to Fort Drum first and then to Fort Pierce. When you and Lester get done covering the graves, I want you to get all the flowers you can find in the woods and put them on your mamma's grave. She liked pretty things, and she'd appreciate you doin' this. And I would too."

Summer

1905

A thunderhead formed in the north as Zech plunged his horse into Turkey Creek, heading for the north corral some five miles from the hammock. He wanted to see the new purebred Hereford bull that had been picked up at the railroad and taken straight to the corral for branding before release on the north range.

He watched the sky, hoping to beat the rain, and soon he came to a small pen off to the left of a barn. Sol and Lester were there, along with the man who replaced Frog, Tim Lardy. Sol watched his father ride up; then he came to him and said, "He's a real beauty, Pappa. He ought to be worth ever cent we paid for him."

Zech walked to the pen and gazed at the polled bull, a sleek creature weighing fifteen hundred pounds, deep red with white splotches on its head and legs, hornless, with a ring in its nose so it could be led easily. Compared to the Brahma that caused death, the Hereford was as gentle as a house cat. It paid no heed as Lester ran a currycomb across its back. The letters "MCI" were freshly burned on its left rear flank.

"He's sure a fine one," Zech said, "and I think you're right, Sol. He's worth the money."

Thunder rumbled across the prairie as lightning flashed in the north, and soon the wind picked up, blowing loose hay from the barn door. Sol said, "Going to rain soon, Pappa. We best head back to the house else we get a drenching."

"You and the rest go on," Zech said. "I'll stay here a short while and ride in after you. I want to look some more. It starts to rain I'll put him in the barn and ride on in as soon as I can."

"All right, Pappa. We'll see you back at the house."

The drive in the summer of 1898 had been the last for MacIvey cattle, and it was the one that set Zech on a new course: raising smaller numbers of quality beeves and giving up on the scrawny yellowhammers. All shipments to market were now made by rail, and the old trails leading to Punta Rassa were a thing of the past, bush-covered but not forgotten.

The year after this final drive, Zech finished fencing all of the MacIvey land, finally putting an end to the fence-cutting by hiring eight men from Arcadia to patrol the property with orders to shoot to kill. After two months on the job and the wounding of five would-be cutters and the killing of two, it all stopped; then the gunslingers rode away.

Twenty thousand acres were eventually put into orange trees, and the other ten thousand used for cattle. Zech upgraded his herd by mixing the range cows with Herefords, gradually breeding his cows to seven-eighths pure Hereford blood; but he never again purchased a Brahma, the bitter memories lingering on.

He made four trips back to Okeechobee to see Toby and also to buy the land where the custard-apple forest was located. For ten thousand five hundred dollars in gold he purchased seventy thousand acres stretching from the lake's southwest shore to the edge of the great cypress swamp. Glenda had been fascinated by his tales of the place and wanted to see it, but he had never taken her there because of the nearby Indian village, fearing that she would somehow learn of Tawanda and Toby. He bought it because of not taking her there, wanting to leave it in its natural state and be sure that no one ever put axes or machines to it, destroying it as the land was destroyed around Palm Beach. He suspected this was also happening at Miami, but he had not returned there to see.

All of the improvements he made to the orange grove and the cattle operation he made for Sol, not for himself. After Glenda's death he had no use for money or any desire for anything except to build something better for Sol, his only remaining link with Glenda and all things past. Surplus money from oranges and cattle still went into trunks stored in the old house.

He also offered to send Sol away to college as he promised Glenda, but the offer was firmly refused. Sol had no interest in further schooling, wanting only to stay on the land and be with his father.

$\mathcal{A}$s the first drops of rain pelted down Zech hooked one finger through the nose ring and led the bull into the barn, guiding it as easily as he would a horse. He put it in a stall with fresh hay; then he went to the door and looked out. The soft shower turned into a downpour, blocking his view of the nearby corral, causing him to retreat further into the barn to escape the pounding water.

Rain always brought memories of Glenda, for some of their happiest times were spent inside the old house, listening to the patter on the cypress roof.

It also reminded him of wildflowers in spring, prairies splashed with green, orange trees bursting with new life, and plains scorched the yellow color of death when it did not come down from cloudless skies.

Black clouds boiled angrily overhead as the rain continued for another hour, tempting him to stay inside the dry barn for a time longer, but knowing that this kind of summer thunderstorm could

131

last well into the night. Sol would be worried, and possibly come out into the storm looking for him, and the worst he could do was soak himself on the return trip.

He mounted his horse and rode away, straining his eyes to see through the rainfall, feeling water pour from the brim of his hat and stream downward inside his shirt.

He soon came to the bank of the creek and gazed across it, seeing that the level had risen two feet, watching brown bubbling foam rush past him as the creek water raced toward the river.

The horse slid and then stumbled as it went down the muddy bank, plunging headlong into the water, causing Zech to be jolted from the saddle as the horse and rider went under and then surfaced a few yards downstream.

Zech thought he had come free, but then he felt a tugging as the horse swam desperately against the current. He knew now that his lame foot was caught in the stirrup, dragging him downward. He held his breath as he went under, trying vainly to free the foot, feeling water rush over him, holding his breath until his lungs could stand it no longer and screamed for mercy; then he let go and sucked for air, pulling a flood of brown water inside him.

Faces and things suddenly rushed through his mind, Tobias and Emma and Glenda and Tawanda and Toby; Ishmael tied to the garden fence, Nip and Tuck baying, Skillit in a clump of palmetto; Frog eating ten biscuits and asking for more; all of them looking at him, calling him to come and be with them; and then he was free, free of the pain in his leg, free of the struggling horse and the rushing water. Sol then came before him, and his last conscious thought was, "Don't grieve, Sol. . . . Don't ever grieve. . . ."

The horse kicked frantically, pulling its load yard by yard across the creek, and when it reached the far bank and struggled upward, Zech's lifeless form dangled from the stirrup.

After resting for a moment the horse started home, moving automatically in the right direction, paying no heed to the saddle pulled sideways by the trailing man, thinking only of the hay stacked in bales in the barn.

Sol was standing on the stoop, beyond reach of the rain, watching, worried because Zech had not yet returned. In a few minutes he would go after him, wishing now he had insisted that his father come back with the rest of them, but not expecting such a flood. Then he saw the horse, moving slowly through the woods, at first seemingly alone; but when it came into the clearing and turned toward the barn, he saw a form being dragged through the mud, the body of a man.

Sol jumped from the stoop screaming, "Pappa! Pappa!"

He could not untangle the foot, so he ran into the house and returned with a knife, cutting the stirrup from the saddle and then carrying Zech inside.

CHAPTER THIRTY-EIGHT

♉

1908

Jessie Lardy, Tim's wife and MacIvey cook and housekeeper for the past eight years, came bustling into the kitchen before sunup. She looked like a white Pearlie Mae, short and overweight, an apron strapped to her, a red bandanna covering her hair.

Sol was sitting at the table, studying a pile of papers in front of him. Jessie put more wood in the stove and said, "I can't sleep when Tim's not here. He should 'a been back two days ago with the load of barrels. He must 'a gone to Jacksonville 'stead of Fort Pierce. I'm goin' to skin that man alive when he gets here!" Then more calmly, "I seen the light and decided I'd come on over. Have you been sittin' there all night, Mister Sol?"

"No, Jessie. I just got up a few minutes ago. I thought I'd go over these deeds and land descriptions one more time before I go."

Jessie picked up the coal oil lamp and looked at it; then she put it back on the table. "That ain't so, Mister Sol! I filled this lamp when I left here last night, and now it's almost empty. You ain't even been to bed. A trip like you got ahead of you today, you ought to have rested. I'll fix us some coffee, and then I'll make breakfast for you."

"Just coffee, Jessie. I'm not hungry."

Jessie put the pot on one lid of the stove and said, "Lordy, Mister Sol, I sure hates to see you leave. I know it's lonely here for a young man like you, without no girls or other young people around. But how come you can't go up to

134

Kissimmee and get yourself a good woman and come on back here to live?"

"It's not that at all," Sol said, pushing the papers aside. "I can stand it being lonely out here, but every time I ride through the woods or go into the grove or tend cows, there's a ghost looking at me. It's like Mamma and Pappa never left. And Grampy and Granny too. I just can't take it any longer, Jessie. I've got to get away from all these faces staring at me. I've got to try something different."

"I understand that, Mister Sol. I just hates to see you go. It won't be the same here without you."

"You'll like the Clayton family. They're good folks. They'll be moving in sometime this afternoon."

Sol had hired a Kissimmee man named Ron Clayton, his wife and three teenaged boys to come live on the place. Clayton would take over as manager of the citrus and cattle operations and be paid a monthly salary plus a percentage of the yearly profits. He had already made several visits to the homestead to study the operation.

Jessie set two cups of coffee on the table. "Maybe so. But they're still not you, Mister Sol."

Sol took a sip of the steaming brew and said, "One thing's for sure, Jessie. I don't have the problem most folks have when they move. There's not much to take with me. Pappa and Grampy had only one suit, and they're buried in them. There's a few dresses of mamma's still in there. You can have them if you want and see if you can let them out and make them fit. I'm taking Grampy's old shotgun and the rifles, Pappa and Grampy's whips, and a few other small things. And that's about it. I'll store it all in the cabin at Punta Rassa. All that stuff's not much for two lifetimes of MacIveys, is it?"

"I guess not, Mister Sol. But they sure left behind a heap more than the mess of junk some folks leave. You can't haul memories in a buckboard, but they're sure there. And they left you enough to last a lifetime."

Lester came in, poured a cup of coffee and sat at the table. Sol noticed how much he had aged so quickly, or perhaps he was just taking a close look at him for the first time. He was as frail and stooped as Frog during his last days.

Sol watched him saucer and blow the coffee, and then he said, "When you get done with that, Lester, I'd appreciate it if you'll go down to the barn and hitch up the buckboard. Put two horses to it, and throw in my saddle. I want to leave soon after sunup."

"Not before you eat!" Jessie said. "I'll fix you a whoppin' big breakfast that'll hold you for a while."

"Coffee's fine, Jessie. I couldn't eat a bite this morning. Honest I couldn't."

"You want me to tie Tiger behind the buckboard?" Lester asked.

"No. He's too old now to go with me. But I want you to see to him real good. Turn him loose in the north range and let him do what he wants to do, and give him plenty to eat. I hate to leave him, but he's just too old. He'll be happy here."

"What about your mamma's horse?"

"Do the same with it." Sol sipped the coffee, and then he said, "I've talked to Clayton about you, Lester, and about Tim and Jessie. All of you have a home here as long as you wish. If it gets to a point where you don't do nothing but tend the garden or just sit on the porch that's fine with me. You'll stay on the payroll. I've told this to Clayton, and he understands. None of you don't ever have to leave unless you want to."

"I appreciate that, Mistuh Sol," Lester said gratefully. "I wouldn't have no idea what to do if I left. We'll all look after things real good. Me and Tim'll keep the graves up like you said, and never let no weeds get to them."

"And I'll put fresh flowers on them ever week," Jessie said. "You don't have to worry about that."

Jessie then started sobbing, and Sol said, "Now stop that, Jessie! I don't want no blubbering. It's hard enough for me to leave as it is. And it's not like I'm going off forever. I'll come back as often as I can to check the books and see how things are going. So you stop that or you'll have me doing it!"

"I couldn't help it, Mister Sol," she said, wiping her eyes. "I won't do it no more."

Lester got up and said, "I'll go on now and bring the buckboard up here, then we'll load your trunk and the other stuff."

Sol was taking one trunk of money with him. The others had been put in one room of Tim and Jessie's cabin and padlocked, Sol cautioning them not to give the key to anyone or let anyone in the room.

Sol followed Lester outside and turned south toward the oak grove and the graves. A dim light was just coming into the hammock, and the eastern sky was tinted red.

He stood before the five stones, all marked MacIvey, two of them covered with wilted flowers. Then he said, "I'm sorry, Pappa, to be leaving, but I just got to go. It's not that I'm afraid to keep on my shoulders what you had to take from Grampy, or what he took himself from the wilderness. I don't know how to explain it, but it's a thing I've got to do.

"And, Mamma, I remember that time you wanted to stay in the fancy hotel at Palm Beach and they wouldn't let Pappa have a room. I'll stay there for you someday, Mamma. I promise you I will.

"Grampy, Granny, Frog–all of you–rest easy. I'll come back to see you again soon."

Then he turned and went back to the house.

As soon as the buckboard arrived they loaded the trunk and the few other things Sol was taking. As he climbed to the seat Jessie said, "God bless you, Mister Sol!"

"You too, Jessie. Tell Tim good-bye for me, and don't be too hard on him because he's late. And, Lester, you take care of yourself. You're about the last old-time cracker left."

The horses trotted away, vanishing quickly in the early morning mist. He headed east first, going to the site of the original corral. When he reached the split-rail fence he stopped and gazed at it, into the empty pen, remembering all those things that had taken place here during his lifetime and before, so much MacIvey blood and sweat and tears staining the ground. The corral was no longer used since there were no more spring roundups of wild cows, but he had given orders to Clayton to maintain it and never tear it down for any reason.

He could almost hear the whips popping and the shouts and the pounding hooves of cows and the smell of scorched flesh as hot irons burned into hides. For a moment he saw it all, thundering out of the mist, becoming alive and real again, then vanishing as suddenly as it appeared. He looked once more, seeing only an empty corral; then he turned the buckboard west toward Punta Rassa and left hurriedly.

☦

CHAPTER THIRTY-NINE

South Okeechobee

1911

The two tracts of land Zech had purchased south of Lake Okeechobee were right in the middle of what was to become the most extensive farmland in South Florida. Sol suspected this when he rode his horse onto the section southeast of the lake and examined the rich soil and the lushness of the vegetation. As he gazed out over the land and then explored it, riding past ponds and sloughs filled with snakes and alligators and turtles, coming to areas of open glades where the shadows of egrets and herons and ibises glided over the sawgrass, his first thought was, "How do you turn a place like this into a farm?"

Upon riding further south he found the answer. Dredges had already worked here for five years, cutting drainage canals across the land, carrying away the water, then using men and machines to strip the land bare and turn it into open fields.

He asked questions everywhere, slowly finding answers, learning who owned the dredges and machines and how much they cost and where to go and whom to see. He built himself a small house on the lake's south shore, and then he set out to transform the land.

He hired dredges to gash the earth and drain it, paying with Spanish gold, then the men and saws and machines to rip out the giant bald cypress and the hickory and the oak and the cabbage palm and the palmetto and the cocoplum bushes, pushing mounds of dirt over the sawgrass and the seas of violet-blue pickerel weed. It took more than a year, but he gradually turned hammocks and Everglades into fields stretching as far as the eye could see, soil so black it looked like soot. Then he formed the MacIvey Produce Company and hired workers to plant tomatoes and beans and squash and celery and corn and cucumbers and lettuce and okra, eventually becoming a supplier of vegetables to the growing cities of Palm Beach and Fort Lauderdale and Miami and Fort Myers and Tampa and Saint Petersburg, also shipping vast quantities by rail to markets in Chicago and New York and Boston.

Then he turned his attention to the land southwest of the lake, attacking the custard-apple forest with more dredges and men and machines, cutting down the ancient trees with their canopies of thick moon vines, ripping out the lush beds of lacy ferns, strewing the ground with thousands of air plants and wild orchids that soon shriveled, burning all of it in huge bonfires that blackened the sky with smoke, slowly transforming jungle into more fields that would put more vegetables onto tables in Palm Beach and Fort Lauderdale and Miami and New York and Boston. Some of this land would also be planted with sugar cane.

Near the end of the clearing of the custard-apple area, Sol decided that since he was so near he would ride down to the Indian village. He had not been there since moving to Okeechobee, and he was sure Toby Cypress did not know about Zech's death and had wondered why Zech never again returned after his last visit seven years ago.

When Sol reached the village it was still as he remembered, the cluster of chickees, the banana trees, a small garden in an open area to the left. Smoke drifted into the thatched roof of one chickee where an old woman tended a cooking pot that smelled of stew.

Sol went to her and said, "I'm looking for Toby Cypress. Do you know where I can find him?"

"His chickee is the last one toward the edge of the woods," she replied, pointing.

A woman in her early twenties was sitting on a cypress stool, operating a foot-pedal Singer sewing machine. Two boys, ages four and two, were playing just outside the chickee. As Sol approached, the woman stopped the machine and watched him. He said, "I'm looking for Toby Cypress."

"I am his wife, Minnie," the woman said, eyeing him curiously. "Could you be Sol MacIvey?"

"Yes, I am," Sol replied, surprised, "How did you know?"

"Toby has spoken of you often. I guessed it because of the hair. He said you have red hair, and we do not see such as that often. Toby is hunting but should return soon. Would you sit here and wait?"

"Yes, I would. I haven't seen Toby in a long time. How is he?"

"He's fine."

"What of Keith Tiger? He was a good friend of my pappa and my grandfather. I could visit with him while I'm waiting."

"Keith Tiger died five years ago."

Sol then became silent, not knowing what more to say and feeling uneasy. He watched for a moment, and then he said, "Are those your boys?"

"Yes. And we will have another in six months. Do you have sons too?"

"No, I don't have any children. I'm not married yet. I've been too busy to give it much thought."

"If you do not marry and have sons, how can you pass on the name of MacIvey?" she asked seriously. "Nothing should be more important to you than that."

The question embarrassed Sol, and he didn't know how to answer since she seemed so concerned about it. He said, "Maybe someday. But I'm glad you and Toby have a family. That's real good. They're part MacIvey, you know."

"Yes, I know."

Toby suddenly came around the side of the banana clump carrying two huge cane cutter rabbits. When he saw Sol beneath the chickee he dropped them and exclaimed, "Sol! How long have you been here? If I had known I would have returned sooner!"

The two of them clasped hands, and Sol said, "I've been here just a short time. I enjoyed visiting with Minnie."

"You have grown into a man since you were here last," Toby said, smiling. "I have to look up to you now, like a pine sapling. But for the red hair, you look exactly like Father. How is he, Sol? I have wondered about him."

"He's dead, Toby. He died six years ago."

"I'm sorry to hear that," Toby said sadly. "But that is why he never returned. How did it happen?"

Both of them sat on the bench, and Sol said, "He was crossing a creek and his horse threw him. His lame foot tangled in the stirrup and he drowned."

"That's too bad. I guess the bad foot must have caused it, for he was the best horse rider I have ever known. He was a good man, Sol, and I hate to know he's gone."

"It hurt me too, real bad, and I was a long time getting over it. But I don't think Pappa hated to go. He never seemed to get over my mamma being killed by a Brahma bull. He blamed himself for it, and after it happened, he didn't really have much interest in anything."

Sol realized immediately he should not talk further about Glenda since the two of them were of different mothers. But before he could change the conversation to something else Toby said, "The stone that Father sent for my mother was brought here since your last visit. Would you like to see it?"

"Yes, I would."

They got up and walked along a path that wound through thick woods and then widened into a clearing surrounded by cabbage palms and pond cypress. Several weathered coffins were on top of the ground and had frames of thin poles built over them. The one stone stood out like a beacon in the middle of the burial ground. Sol walked to it and gazed at the words:

Tawanda MacIvey

Beloved

He finally said, "It's real nice, Toby. Real nice. I'm glad Pappa did this."

"It is a fine stone," Toby said proudly. "I come here often to look. Mother would be pleased with the name Father put on it."

They went back to the chickee and again sat on the bench. Toby said, "Are you still raising cattle at your ranch on the Kissimmee?"

"Yes, but I don't live there anymore. I left a man in charge of it and moved to the south shore of Okeechobee three years ago."

"You've been so close by for three years and haven't come here?" Toby questioned. "Why is this, Sol? We could have hunted and fished together like we once did."

"I wanted to, but I've been too busy. Pappa owned two sections of land below the lake, and I've been clearing them for farming. We're working up north of here now."

Toby's eyes flashed surprise. He said, "You mean it is you who is destroying the land? I cannot believe this, Sol. Father would have never put an ax to the custard-apple trees. He loved that place. Why is it you are doing this?"

Sol was shocked by the reaction. He said, "Like I said, Toby, I'm turning it into farm land. People in the new cities have to eat, and there's beginning to be more and more of them. I'm growing vegetables in the fields."

"Animals have to eat too, and so do birds, and so do we!" Toby said angrily. "Will your machines not stop until they come here and crush my mother's grave? I hope they never enter this swamp, or go into Pay-Hay-Okee. If they do, you will have destroyed us too, all of us!"

Sol was totally dumbfounded, wishing he had never mentioned his work. He said, "It's just swamp, Toby. And there's plenty more of it."

"It is not just swamp!" Toby responded harshly. "It is God you are killing. He put the land here for all creatures to enjoy, and you are destroying it. When you destroy the land you destroy God. Do you not know this? Go now and stand in the middle of your fields. Count the deer you see, and the alligators, and the fish, and the birds. Count them, Sol, and then tell me how many are still there. You have crushed them with your machines, and if you do not stop what you are doing, there will soon be no more! They will be gone forever!"

Sol got up and said, "I'm sorry you feel this way, Toby. But it's my land now, and I have the right to do whatever I want with it."

"You are a traitor to the wishes of your father!" Toby snapped, his face now flushed red with anger. "He told me himself he purchased the custard-apple forest so no one could ever put an ax to it, and you have leveled it to the ground! He would die a second death if he knew this!"

"He told you that?" Sol asked, surprised. "He never said anything like that to me."

"Why should he? He never dreamed you would someday come down here and do what you have done. Wasn't the cattle ranch enough for you to make money? Where will you go from here with your machines? I am no longer proud to call you brother!"

Sol couldn't take it any longer. "I'm really sorry you said that, Toby. I've only done what I thought was right, but no matter what a person does, he can't please everybody. Someone will object. I'm sorry." Then he mounted his horse and rode out of the village.

As soon as he was gone Minnie Cypress said, "You were too cruel to him, Toby. After all, he is your half-brother."

"I had to be," Toby replied, "and it hurt me more than it did him. I only hope it makes him think. But I suppose it cannot be blamed on Sol. If it were not him doing this, it would be someone else. And many others will follow. I hate to think of the end of it."

Sol felt sick as he rode back through the swamp, thinking of what Toby said about the custard-apple forest, the word "traitor" still ringing in his ears. Since Zech had never mentioned this to him, he could not be sure Toby's words were true. And it was natural that anyone living off the land like Toby and his people would feel the way Toby did. Toby would soon forget it, he told himself, and they would become friends again. And what little land he had cleared would not make that much difference anyway. There was much of it left, more than anyone could ever use. He vowed he would go back someday and try to make peace with Toby.

Sol got up at dawn the next morning, still shaken from Toby's words. He paced back and forth for several minutes, muttering. Then he went into the kitchen and made coffee.

He was hungry, but he did not want to fry eggs and eat alone again. He ate one piece of stale white bread with the coffee; then he started pacing again.

It was Saturday, and all the field hands and work crews had left for the weekend. He thought first of going fishing, but this too was no fun alone. Many times on lonely nights and weekends he wished he had never left the homestead, where at least he would have Lester and Tim and Jessie. One of the reasons for leaving was to escape the loneliness, but instead he had trapped himself in a situation far worse than the one he left.

There was nothing in the nearby villages of Clewiston and Belle Glade but a few stores and small cafés where he often took evening meals to escape the boredom of cooking for himself. He longed for one of his mother's meals or one prepared by Jessie, good wholesome food and not something always fried in stale grease that should have been dumped long ago. The villages were also empty of people his age.

He went into the bedroom, put on fresh jeans and a denim jacket, and attempted to dust off his boots; then he went outside and got into one of the Ford Model T trucks he had bought for delivering vegetables. The motor sputtered to life, shaking the fenders as if they would fall off; then he put it in gear and started off, the rutted sand road causing it to rattle even worse.

There was a dirt road leading directly east from Belle Glade, crossing forty-seven miles of prairie into West Palm Beach. He pointed the Model T in that direction and floored the accelerator, sounding like an approaching hurricane as he roared across the land. Terrified rabbits jumped six feet high as they bounded out of his path, competing with frightened deer that almost trampled the smaller animals as they rushed past them. Birds flew too, and buzzards circled overhead, watching all of it, sensing there would soon be some kind of disaster that provided food.

When he reached West Palm Beach he sped right through it, scattering chickens and cats and dogs, stirring up a cloud of dust until he hit the wooden bridge leading across the water to Palm Beach proper. The accelerator was still on the floor as he drove straight to the driveway of the Royal Poinciana Hotel, came to a screeching halt in front of the main entrance, and jumped out. A cloud of blue smoke drifted across the veranda, and steam made angry hissing sounds as it boiled from beneath the truck's hood.

The doorman came down the steps hurriedly, eyeing the 'MacIvey Produce Company' sign on the dusty truck's door. He commanded Sol, "Get that thing out of here! Are you crazy? All deliveries are made at the rear entrance! Move it, fellow!"

Sol glared back, and then he said, "I'm not delivering anything! I'm a customer, and I want a room here for the weekend! And you best let the truck sit right here till I go in and inquire about it!"

The doorman stared as Sol stalked off.

Sol crossed the lobby briskly, going straight to the counter, popping his hand several times on a little bell. A man in a white linen suit came from behind a shelf of key boxes and said, "Something I can do for you?"

"I want a room," Sol said, "one with a view of the ocean if you've got it. Otherwise, I'll take anything."

The clerk looked first at the jeans and denim jacket, at the boots with mud caked to the soles; then he examined a ledger briefly and said, "If you don't have a confirmed reservation we're all full. And I assume you don't."

"That's right, I don't," Sol replied, taking a thick roll of bills from his pocket. "You folks pulled that reservation stuff on my pappa when my mamma wanted to stay here. I don't have a reservation, but I've got enough money here to choke a stallion. You going to give me a room or not?"

"I've already told you," the man said. "We're full up."

"O.K.," Sol said, putting the money back into his pocket. "My name is MacIvey. Sol MacIvey. I want you to remember that. One of these days I'll build my own hotel, and it'll be a heap sight better than this dump."

As Sol turned away the man said, "Cracker hick!"

When he got back to the truck he drove it off the driveway and right down the middle of a flowerbed, scattering plants in all directions, hearing the doorman run after him screaming.

It was an hour past noon when he got back into West Palm Beach, and he parked in front of a café, got out and went inside. It was nothing fancy but clean, with good smells coming from the kitchen. Tables were covered with checkered cloths, and several people, obviously workers from their dress, were finishing eating.

A waitress came over and handed Sol a menu. She appeared to be about twenty, with long blonde hair and blue eyes. She would be pretty except for the sour look on her face.

Sol said, "I'll have the blue plate special."

He paused for a moment, and then he said, "You know, you'd be as pretty as a speckled calf if you'd just smile."

She did smile, and then she said, "Thanks. Most folks never give me a compliment. They just gripe about how slow the service is, and I do the best I can. But you don't look like mister sunshine yourself. You came bustin' in here like a thunderhead."

"I guess I did," Sol said, chuckling. "I had a bad experience over in Palm Beach, and it sort of got my dander up."

"It's not hard to do over there. I stay away from that place."

Sol said, "What's your name?"

"Bonnie."

"Bonnie what?"

"Bonnie O'Neil. My daddy is Irish."

"I'm Sol MacIvey. My daddy was cracker."

"Cracker?" she giggled. "What's that?"

"Men who run after cows crackin' whips. That's how come they're called crackers."

"Is that what you do, run after cows?"

"I used to, but I'm in the vegetable business now."

"We got a garden too, but Daddy won't put a hand to it. He makes me do all the work. Where's your place?"

"Over at Lake Okeechobee."

She glanced back toward the kitchen and said, "I better get your food before Mister Lumkin comes shouting at me. I'll be right back."

When she returned Sol said, "What time you get off work here?"

"Two o'clock. You're the last customer for the noon serving. But I have to come back at five and work another two hours."

"You want to go over to the beach for awhile?"

"And do what?" she asked.

"Sit. We could gawk at the men in their knickers, like they do us. After that I'll have to go on back to Okeechobee. I don't like to be on the road at night. If my truck broke down the skeeters would eat me alive."

"Sure, why not. It would beat going home and washing clothes. I'll meet you a block down the street. Mister Lumkin would have a stroke if he saw me leave here with a customer. He doesn't allow that at all."

They sat on the small area of public beach, watching waves roll in from the ocean and sandpipers scurrying about, pecking frantically at the sand as the water rushed back. Sol said, "Those little birds sure are swift. They never get their feet wet. Reminds me of a wild bull when you trap him in a palmetto clump. You never know which way he's going to go."

"Mamma used to like to come here and watch the birds. She's dead now. Died three years ago."

"What does your pappa do?" Sol asked.

"He's a groundskeeper at the hotel. Mamma worked there too, in the kitchen, till she took sick. Since she died Daddy don't do nothing but drink. I have to cook all the meals and do the washing and cleaning and tend the garden. When Daddy gets home from work he's drunk before supper."

"If you have to do all that, how come you work in the café too?"

"Daddy makes me. He wants the money, an' he takes all of it. He won't even give me a dollar. If I get a tip I hide it in my shoe so he can't find it."

Sol became silent for a moment, thinking, and then he said, "How much you make at that café?"

"Twenty dollars a month."

"Would you like to change jobs?"

"I sure would, but there's nowhere else for me to go. Those people won't hire me in their fancy shops, and I don't want to work at the hotel. I tried that once. I had to clean twenty rooms every day."

"That's not what I mean," Sol said. "How'd you like to come and work for me?"

"Doing what?" she asked, surprised.

"I need someone to do the cooking and look after the house. I'm tired of being alone and having to do all of the housework myself. I'll pay you a hundred dollars a month."

She turned to him and said, "A hundred dollars a month? I've never seen that much money. How much of a garden have you got if you can pay a hundred dollars a month for a cook?"

"A hundred and thirty thousand acres. And a good bit more at other places."

"Oh, my!" she exclaimed, not knowing whether to believe him or not. But he said it too matter-of-factly to be lying. Then she said, "If you're so tired of being alone, how come you haven't married? It would be a whole lot cheaper than hiring a cook at that price."

"Pappa told me once that getting married is like owning dogs. You get to liking them too much, and it pains you when they go away. I saw it happen to Grampy when my granny died, and then to Pappa too. It pained them both worse than I've ever seen. I'm just not sure yet I want to try it. Maybe someday. You'll be just a housekeeper. But we need to start to Okeechobee now. You want to go and tell your daddy, or what?"

"No way!" she said, still not sure to believe what was happening. "He'd beat me. He's done it before, and I don't want any more of it. He doesn't work Saturday afternoons, so he's home now. I can't even get my clothes."

"Don't worry about that," Sol said, getting up. "I've got enough money with me to buy out a store. We'll stop and get whatever you need."

As they walked back to the truck Bonnie said, "I don't believe this! It's just not real. I thought I'd never get out of that café. You don't know how many times I've thought about running away to Miami or Jacksonville but didn't have the nerve to do it. And here you come out of nowhere, and suddenly I'm gone. Just like that. I don't believe it's really happening to me."

"It's real, Bonnie," Sol said. "I wish I had found you a long time ago. The moment I saw you in the café I knew I wanted to do this. I was afraid you'd turn me down."

She stopped momentarily and said, "You know, Sol, you're a real nice fellow. I mean it. I'm sure glad you stopped at the café."

"I am too, Bonnie. You're the kind of girl my mamma would like. I'll take you to our homestead sometime. It's up on the Kissimmee River. You'll like it."

"I already do."

"We best get on the way," Sol said, smiling. "That truck stops after dark, the skeeters'll suck us dry."

"Then let's go!" she said.

🐂

1918

The Ford car bounced along the road leading past the east shore of the lake, swerving when it hit sand pockets. Sol said, "If it wasn't for saving time, I'd rather be going up there on a horse. It's a lot smoother."

"Does seem a bit rough," Bonnie replied, almost shouting over the roar of the engine. "But I'd never make it that far on a horse. I don't know how you stood it when you drove those cows clear across the state."

"Sometimes I don't either. I guess I was tougher then, and surely a lot younger. But I'd like to do it one more time just for the heck of it. I remember when it took us three days to move cows as far as we can go in one hour with this flivver. But we weren't in any hurry and didn't know the difference."

"Are we going back by Punta Rassa?"

"Yes. I want to check on the cabin and see if they got the fence done like I ordered."

"When you come to a nice shady hammock we can stop and have a picnic. I've brought a real nice lunch."

"There's one just past Basinger," Sol said. "We've got to get to the place by early afternoon. I've got a lot to do there before we go on to Punta Rassa."

"That letter has really upset you, hasn't it?"

"Tim Lardy would never have written me twice to come back in a hurry unless something is bad wrong. I should have gone after the first letter. But I'm anxious to get there now and find out what it is that's got Tim in such a stew."

Bonnie was a housekeeper, but she was also a companion. She became Sol's business partner as well, doing all the clerical work and offering advice when Sol was in doubt about what he was doing. And her advice always proved right.

For several years after Sol left the homestead he went back every few months to check things out, but as the vegetable business continued to grow and prosper and demand more and more of his time, the visits became less frequent.

On one of his visits he loaded the remaining money trunks on a Model T truck and took them to his house at Okeechobee, and this also made it seem less necessary for him to go back on a regular schedule.

It had been over two years since he was at the homestead, handling all business matters by mail. This had not bothered him, for the old place produced more and more cash income, and Clayton's books were always in order. But a year ago Clayton wrote him that he was going into business for himself at Bartow and recommended that a man named Donovan replace him as manager. He assured Sol that Donovan was experienced with both citrus and cattle, so Sol hired Donovan by mail.

Sol had no reason to doubt his decision, for the income from the place continued to increase steadily. Then came the first letter from Tim Lardy, urging him to come back as soon as possible. He knew he should have gone at once, but he put it off for one thing and then another. And than a second letter arrived, this one even more urgent. At this point Sol dropped everything, and he and Bonnie set out immediately, Sol regretful that he had not responded sooner.

Sol turned from the main road and followed a trail leading across a section of prairie, the tall grass making swishing sounds as it brushed the underside of the vehicle. When he came to an area that should have been open pasture but was now an orange grove it confused him, thinking perhaps he had taken the wrong turn.

He stopped for a moment and said, "I know this is where the corral was. We never planted trees here. Something is powerful strange, Bonnie."

"Are you sure we're at the right place?" she asked.

"I think so, unless I've gone crazy. Let's go on to the house and see what this is all about."

He continued following the trail and became even more confused when he arrived at the spot where he thought the hammock would be but found only more orange trees. He began to wonder if he really had come to the right place, but at the same time doubting he could have forgotten so soon.

Bonnie remained in the car as Sol started walking through the grove, searching for some sign of recognition, startled once when a rabbit bounded from a clump of grass right at his feet and rushed away. And then he came to it, right in the middle of two rows of trees, five stones, all bearing the name MacIvey. He stared for a moment, at once not believing, then realizing what had been done. He screamed furiously, "You no good son of a gun! I'll get you!"

The sound of it frightened Bonnie so badly she jumped from the car, trembling as Sol rushed from the trees and slid beneath the steering wheel. She climbed back in quickly, her eyes terrified as Sol cranked the car and spun it around, going full speed back down the trail, crashing into limbs and showering the air with twigs and leaves.

His hands gripped the wheel. They skidded sideways when the trail split with another path leading off to the left. The Ford righted itself and roared forward again, the motor straining and leaving a trail of blue smoke.

Soon he came to a small clearing containing a house and two

small cabins off to one side, all of them new and made of pine. The car skidded to a stop and spun around, facing back the way it had come.

A cloud of dust boiled up as Sol jumped from the car and grabbed a Winchester from the back seat. Tim and Jessie then came from one cabin, and as soon as they recognized who it was, Jessie started crying.

Tim ran forward and said, "I couldn't stop him, Mistuh Sol! I tried, but he wouldn't listen to me!"

Donovan came around the side of the house, trotting, drawn by the sound of the unexpected commotion. He was a huge man, six and a half feet tall, gruff-looking, built like an ox. Sol knew who he was without being told. He cocked the lever of the Winchester, pointed it and said, "I'm going to blow your head off!"

Donovan froze, looking at the trembling hand pressing the trigger, the barrel pointed directly at him, the rage in Sol's eyes. He spoke as calmly as possible, "You must be Mister MacIvey. How come you're in such a huff?"

"What you mean by what you've done?" Sol demanded, hatred for this unknown man pouring from him like sweat.

"I don't know what you mean."

"You know!" Sol shouted, his face now as red as his hair.

"Them houses was rotting down," Donovan said, still looking at the rifle and not at Sol. "They wasn't worth nothin'. And there's three hundred acres of good land where that hammock was. I was hired to run a grove on a percentage basis, not look after some old shacks and run a old-folks home. You ought to be glad I cleared off all that stuff and put it in oranges. It'll mean more money for you."

Bonnie had never seen Sol so angry, and she knew he was going to do it. She ran to him and pleaded, "Please, Sol, don't! What's done is done, and killing him won't bring it back! It'll only bring trouble! Please listen to me!"

He looked at her terrified face, then back to Donovan, and then he said, "I want you off this place in ten minutes! You get in that truck over there and go! Whatever you leave behind we'll burn! Now move it and count yourself lucky! If you're still here in ten minutes, so help me, I'll kill you!"

Sol watched as Donovan went into the house and then came outside dragging a frightened woman by the arm. He did not lower the rifle until the truck sputtered down the trail and disappeared.

Tim then said, "I tried to stop him, Mistuh Sol! He just wouldn't pay no mind to me at all!"

"What'd he do with my granny's cook stove?" Sol asked.

"He give to a junk man from St. Cloud. All the old tools and other stuff too."

Sol looked around and said, "Where's Lester?"

"Over in his cabin. He don't work anymore, Mistuh Sol. He's been too poorly. Mistuh Donovan was goin' to run him off the place, and he would have too if you hadn't come right now."

Sol tried to calm himself and think, but the anger wouldn't go away. He said, "I can't stay here any longer today or I'll go after him and kill him for sure. Tim, I want you to take over as manager and run the place from now on."

Tim's eyes widened, and then he said, "Mistuh Sol, I appreciate your saying that. I know the orange and cattle business as good as anybody, but I'm sure not a bookkeeper. I just couldn't handle that part of it at all."

"It doesn't matter. I'll hire a bookkeeper in Kissimmee to come here once a month and take care of that. That's not important, but running the place is. And you can do it, Tim. The first thing I want you to do is rip out all those trees where the graves are. Clear it all out, and then put an iron fence around it. And plant some oak back in there."

"I'll do it, Mistuh Sol. It near 'bout killed me and Jessie when he done that. We knowed how you'd feel, but I just couldn't stop him."

"We're going to go now," Sol said, his voice still trembling. "I'll go to Kissimmee and talk to a bookkeeper, and I'll also hire a couple of hands to come live here and work under you. I'll come back in about a month and help you set things up."

"I'll do a good job for you, Mistuh Sol. And I'll see to the grave site right away."

Without speaking further Sol got into the car and drove off. When he reached the place where the corral had been he stopped, leaned forward against the steering wheel and cried bitterly.

He finally straightened up and controlled himself, and then he said, "You know, Bonnie, he bulldozed two whole lifetimes. Everything Pappa and Grampy did is gone now. It's a wonder he didn't pull out the stones and plant trees there too. I should have stayed here and looked after the place. Those vegetable fields aren't worth this. It's all my fault."

"That's not true, Sol," she insisted, feeling the pain with him. "You couldn't have known this would happen."

A shocked realization came on Sol's face as something unexpected came into his mind. He suddenly understood why Toby had been so angry when he destroyed the custard-apple forest, a place that both Zech and Toby loved. To them it was much more than just another stretch of raw swamp and forest. And he had done the same thing Donovan had done, only it was for vegetables rather than oranges.

He brushed his eyes and said, "They'll never forgive me for this, Bonnie, and I know I won't forgive myself. All they left behind is gone now, and regrets won't bring it back. Toby knew this, and now I do too. Toby was right and I was wrong, but it's done now, and what's done can't be undone. I guess nothing in this whole stinking world lasts forever."

She did not know who Toby was, and none of it made sense to her. She passed it off as rambling grief, but the puzzled look stayed on her face as he cranked the car and drove off. When he reached a turn in the trail he stopped and glanced back briefly just to be sure the old corral was really gone.

✝

CHAPTER FORTY-ONE

1924

After moving to Okeechobee, Sol made many trips into Miami selling his produce. On his first visit in 1908 the place did not even look like the sleepy little village he and Zech and Glenda rode into that summer day in 1895. The coming of Flagler's railroad, which arrived the next year, changed the face of the area. With each visit Sol found something new.

He made no plans whatsoever for the land they owned there, merely paying the taxes each year and letting the vegetation grow wild. Twice he bought other small plots and threw the deeds into a box with the others. During one early visit he did hire a skiff and cross the bay to see his beachside property—a mangrove swamp occupied by chattering birds and roaming animals, the beach itself a haven for sandpipers and gulls and terns and pelicans.

In January of 1912 Sol and Bonnie went into Miami and bought tickets on the first train to run from Miami to Key West over Flagler's overseas railroad, seeing the old man himself dressed in a black frock coat and silk stovepipe hat, the two of them staying in Key West for a four-day celebration. The whole island was one big party. They were both exhausted when they arrived back in Miami and then returned gladly to the calm life of their Okeechobee home.

Sol and Bonnie watched from the sidelines as Miami grew, and waited, frightened by all of it, Sol knowing that day by day and week by week his property became more valuable. Each rumor and each newspaper ad and circular listing land values stunned him, and he knew he would have to do something, but he continued to wait.

In 1923 he made his first move, hiring a contractor to build a house and office in Miami, the first floor to be the business area and the second floor the living quarters. It was a small place compared to the Spanish-style mansions rapidly dotting the area, the ten-story office buildings and the vast hotels and apartments.

Sol built his house as if building a fort, with foot-thick concrete walls and iron grills across each window. One of the first-level rooms contained a walk-in vault, the same type as in a bank. The contractor thought Sol was crazy, warning him that such a vault located inside a house would probably cost as much as the house itself.

His reason for this unusual addition was that he would keep his money himself, just as his father and grandfather had done, and trust no bank or anyone else with it. Had it not been for the MacIvey system of banking by trunk, as started by Tobias and continued by Zech, there might not have been any MacIvey land and no reserve money to purchase more or to develop what he now had. Sol figured what was good for them was good for him, only his new trunk would be a great deal stronger than the steamers purchased by Tobias in Punta Rassa. He soon owned the only house in Miami with a full-sized steel and concrete vault, and from the outside appearance of his place, no one else would know it was there.

As soon as the house-office was complete Sol hired a foreman for the vegetable business and set forth to participate in the great Florida Boom. The sign outside his office read, "MacIvey Real Estate and Development Company."

After having it surveyed, Sol found that the six thousand acres of Miami property covered a portion of the commercial area of the city and extended into one of the most sought-after residential areas, including waterfront. None of it was swamp or muckland, so there would be no need of drainage or filling before placing it on the market. He plotted only a small section at first just to see what would happen, breaking an acre into individual lots of seventy feet by one hundred feet. Then he studied current prices listed by other firms, finding that lots ranged from twenty to seventy thousand dollars according to location. The Miami Beach acreage was even more valuable. He could not believe that people would actually pay so much money for land.

By the end of a month they loaded a car with suitcases and set forth for the peaceful country, leaving behind over $80 million in their Miami vault.

CHAPTER FORTY-TWO

September 15, 1928

Sol turned left at Belle Glade and headed for Lake Harbor and the Okeechobee house. It was Saturday, and they had driven up from Miami that morning, leaving the city because of advance warnings that a hurricane was approaching from the south. Memories were still too fresh of what had happened in Miami and Miami Beach two years before when a September hurricane virtually destroyed the area, bringing an end to the great frenzied land boom.

Sol and Bonnie had ridden that one out in their little concrete house, coming out unhurt into a city littered with the trash of scattered houses, flattened hotels and apartment buildings, the harbor blocked by sunken vessels, forty-foot yachts resting on dry land a half mile inland. People had wandered the streets dazed, not believing that the great Florida Sun God could do this to them, seeing all their hopes and dreams swept away by the shrieking winds and surging tides.

Sol and Bonnie were not hurt by it, and were in fact helped. A week later they put a sign in front of their office saying, "We're Buying."

Sol purchased property after property, believing that someday the area would recover, because he knew of all those things the

MacIveys had suffered—worse than this—and come back again and again, refusing to surrender.

But they wanted no more of a Miami-style hurricane and the sturdy old cypress house at Lake Okeechobee offered a safe haven out of the path of whatever was coming.

They stopped at a country store and purchased supplies, making sure the house was well stocked with food for at least a week's stay if that was necessary. After the suitcases and bags of groceries were put in the house, Sol set out alone to inspect some of his fields.

When Sol returned to the house, he and Bonnie drove along a sandy trail leading to the lake, passing cabbage palm hammocks strangely without birds, huge oaks whose limbs were normally playgrounds for barking squirrels now empty and silent. As he rounded a bend there was an area of open sawgrass off to the left, and the air above the marsh churned with white specks so thick they formed a low-lying cloud.

Sol stopped the car, and they both gazed at it. Bonnie then said, "What is it, Sol? Is it insects?"

"No, it's pollen," Sol replied. "It's not a good sign, either. Toby Cypress once told me that when sawgrass pollen boils like that it means a great storm is coming. They flee from the sight of it. Maybe it's just another Indian legend, but it's weird, isn't it?"

"Yes, and I don't want to look anymore," Bonnie said, suddenly shivering. "It still looks like bugs to me, and I don't want to be around it."

Sol drove on, and then he parked on the bank of a drainage canal leading eastward from the lake. Flights of herons and egrets and ibises were streaming above the water, moving northward, not floating casually as they often do with wings outspread, but flapping constantly.

The surface of the lake was deathly still, like a mirror tying together an immediate point with the horizon. In the distance they could see commercial fishermen taking their boats toward the mouth of a creek.

They both got out of the car and walked along the canal, watching small explosions as bass struck minnows lurking at the edges of pickerel weed. Then there was a more violent upheaval as an alligator snapped up one of the stalking bass, chomping it into a bloody pulp and then gliding away, its powerful tail weaving slowly, sending ripples against the bank.

"That's the way it goes," Sol said as the 'gator disappeared into a clump of weeds. "Minnow eats the skeeter eggs, bass eats the minnow, 'gator eats the bass, and next thing you know he ends up as shoes and belts, his tail meat in somebody's frying pan."

"I feel sorry for the poor fish," Bonnie said. "I sure wouldn't want to be chomped up like that."

"Neither does the minnow, but nothing has a choice. Everything has to eat, Bonnie, including us. And we all eat each other. If we'd brought along our poles we could have a fish fry tonight, the way those bass are striking."

"I've got steaks," Bonnie replied. "I don't want fish after watching that. And if you don't hush up that kind of talk you won't get anything. You make me feel like a cannibal."

"I hope you don't think the cow those steaks came from committed suicide," Sol grinned. "But we won't go into that. I'll hush."

They walked a short distance further, and then Sol said, "I've never seen the lake so still, and the birds all moving in one direction. I've got a gut feeling something is wrong here, bad wrong."

"I do too," Bonnie said. "It's eerie. Maybe we should have stayed in Miami."

"One thing for sure," Sol said, slapping his arms, "the skeeters aren't leaving too. Let's get out of here before they have us for supper."

As they drove back past the stretch of marsh, the pollen boiled even more, looking like millions of swarming gnats. Sol stopped briefly and looked again, saying, "If Toby were here he'd be cutting out for somewhere else. Next thing you know an owl will light on our roof and cry out. That's an even worse omen."

"Quit kidding me," Bonnie said, her voice serious. "This place is spooky enough without you scaring me worse with Indian tales. I don't want to hear any more of it."

The sun did not come up the next morning. Instead, it seeped through leaden skies that rapidly turned from gray to angry black, boiling like the pollen boiled. At first the wind came in gusts, banging against the side of the house and causing palm trunks to bend double and then snap back. By mid-morning it changed to a steady howl, bringing with it a sheet of pelting rain that came in horizontally, pinging sharply against the walls and windowpanes.

Sol looked out one of the east windows and noticed that the door on the garage had come open. It flapped back and forth violently, as rapidly as blades on a windmill, shaking the structure on its foundation. When he opened the front door of the house to go out to the garage, the door slammed back with such force it knocked him sprawling across the floor, snapping one steel hinge like it was made of matchsticks. He and Bonnie put their shoulders against the door and forced it back, and then he nailed it shut.

Bonnie backed away exhausted, soaked instantly from rain that rushed through the open space and splattered against the living room walls. She said, "I'm afraid, Sol. Really afraid! What are we going to do?"

"There's nothing we can do," Sol said, picking up the hammer and nails. "I'll nail every door and window shut and then pray the old house holds together. Looks like we jumped right out of it in Miami and landed in the path up here."

"I wish we'd stayed there," Bonnie moaned. "We could have got inside the vault and been safe."

The house cracked and vibrated constantly as Sol put his arms around Bonnie and tried to reassure her. "Don't worry. We'll make it through this. We always have, and we will again."

"I hope so," Bonnie replied. "But Lord, I don't know, Sol! I just wish it would go away."

They ate cold beans for lunch, and shortly afterwards Sol looked out the window just as the banging garage came apart, pieces of walls and roof sailing upward and disappearing, exposing the car to the full force of the wind. It bounced up and down like a rubber ball, skipping across the ground a few feet at a time, and then it rolled over and over and crashed into a clump of palm trunks.

By mid-afternoon the area outside the house was covered with brown foam as the lake water reached the yard. Waves on the lake gradually increased, starting at two feet and going to six, crashing over the flat banks and rushing southward; and then it came like tidal waves, ten feet high, wall after wall of wind-driven water, uprooting palms and oaks and anything in its way. It inched up the house's foundation, three feet off the ground, then it touched the porch floor and slushed in beneath the doors.

Bonnie stared with horror as the water covered the floor, an inch at first and then three inches, rising rapidly. She wailed, "Oh my, Sol! What can we do? The whole lake is coming down on us!"

"Stand on a chair!" Sol shouted above the roar. "It can't come higher than that!"

But it did come higher, lapping the top of the dining room table. Then Sol put a chair on top of the table and climbed through an opening into the roof rafters, pulling Bonnie after him, the two of them clinging to studs as cypress shingles gave way and sailed off like leaves, exposing them to the pounding rain that made breathing almost impossible.

And then it stopped suddenly, as instantly as if someone had flicked off a light switch, the night now deathly still, not a single drop of rain coming down. Sol looked up through a hole in the roof, seeing the moon and stars trapped inside a swirling mass shaped like an inverted ice cream cone, one big round area of peaceful sky surrounded by spinning madness. He said, "It's the eye, Bonnie. It's passing over us now. Are you still all right?"

She pulled herself across the stud to him, sucking air into her tortured lungs. "I don't know, Sol," she gasped. "I can't hang on here much longer. And we're only half way through it. It's coming again, only this time worse! I don't know what we'll do."

"I'll hold you," Sol responded, putting his arms around her soggy body. "We'll make it, Bonnie. We have to! Just don't give up."

Water sloshed two feet below them.

The first gust then struck the house, coming from the opposite direction of the previous wind, signaling the passing of the eye and the coming of the second phase. It increased rapidly, now roaring, rain coming again and pounding through the open roof, making further talk impossible.

Sol shuddered with fear and clung desperately to Bonnie as he felt the house being jolted from its foundation, moving off slowly, pushed along by surging water as the lake left its banks again and pounded southward. And then it exploded, sounding like a dynamite charge, sending boards and beams and window frames flying away with the howling wind. Sol felt himself ripped from Bonnie and flipped over and over like a coin, splashing down into angry, boiling water, gasping for breath as he went under and came back up again, grabbing frantically in utter darkness for something to hold to, finally locking his aching arms onto a section of roof as it swept by. His shouts of "Bonnie! . . . Bonnie! . . ." were heard only by himself as he moved rapidly over what had once been a vegetable field.

*D*awn came from a sky still gray, but the violence was gone. Rain pelted down steadily as Sol opened his eyes and looked up.

The roof section had come to rest against a drainage canal dike, and above him he could hear voices as a group of black field hands sang gospel hymns and prayed. The water was clogged with the remains of shattered houses and trees, and the floating bodies of dead animals and humans. A small child was jammed into the fork of a tree limb just to the left of Sol.

He pushed away from the beams and pulled himself slowly up the muddy bank, at first unable to stand, kneeling and looking out across a brown sea. Not a tree was left standing, not a house or barn, nothing visible but water covering the earth as far as he could see. One of the field hands watched him for a moment, and then he said, "Bless you, brother, bless you! Praise the Lord for bein' spared!" And then he returned to the hymn.

Sol stared at the man blankly. Then he pushed himself up and staggered forward, seeing people further down the dike, his blistered eyes searching for some sign of a small woman wearing a blonde ponytail. He cried out, "Bonnie! . . . Where are you, Bonnie?"

But there was no answer, and never would be. Bonnie was among the two thousand who had died and vanished forever.

Miami

1954

$\mathcal{S}$ol sat behind the massive mahogany desk in his office atop the MacIvey State Bank, waiting impatiently for the woman to keep her appointment. He did not want to go through with this, thinking it foolish. The call came the day before, from the executive director of the Greater Miami Economic Council, telling him he had been selected Citizen of the Year for his lifetime contributions to the Miami area and to Florida. But so little was known about his private life, which he guarded, they had requested an interview to gain information for publicity and for the award ceremony to be held the next week.

Finally she was brought in, a young woman of twenty-two, with deep green eyes and black hair, wearing shoes with spikes four inches tall. She was nervous as she took a seat in front of the desk.

She took a note pad and pen from her purse and said, "I'm Alice Bryant, Mister MacIvey. I've always wanted to meet you but never thought I would. And I want to congratulate you on the honor. You certainly deserve it for all you've done for the state."

"Just what is it you want to know?" Sol asked, bored already as he leaned back in the chair.

"Oh, just everything," she replied. "Something about your

family background, how you got your start, where you went to school. All that sort of thing."

Sol's eyes suddenly twinkled with laughter as he said, "O.K., Miss Bryant. I'll talk, and you take notes. Then you can ask questions. First, my granddaddy was a plantation owner in Georgia and came to Florida before the Civil War to establish a cattle and citrus empire. He served as a Confederate general during the war. My pappa helped Grampy buy the land and start the business, and I learned it from them. But before I took it over and expanded it, I was sent away to college. Graduated from the University of Virginia in 1906, with honors. My mother was from a pioneer family too, and so was my wife. She died back in 1928. My wife's father was one of the founders of Palm Beach. . . . Now the way we really started the MacIvey empire was. . . . "

The Okeechobee hurricane of 1928 changed the face of the land forever. As Sol vowed that morning as he searched for Bonnie, the lake was eventually diked, surrounded by such a high mound of dirt that its waters would never again be seen from ground level. Then drainage canals were cut, drying up the muck soil until summer winds blew it away, turning the life-giving water away from the Big Cypress Swamp and the Everglades, creating drought in dry seasons when the natural flow from the lake no longer came, and flooding in rainy seasons because the earth could no longer absorb it. It was all done with good intent and faith at the time but nevertheless created a terrible wrong against nature that could never be reversed.

Sol played a big part in it because of his anger at the storm and Bonnie's death. He rebuilt the Okeechobee house, this time of concrete and steel, and then he went back to Miami. When the Depression came in 1929, causing banks to fail, he started his own, naming it the MacIvey State Bank and stocking it with hard cash from his private vault.

His MacIvey Development Company continued buying land during the 1930s, moving up the coast and inward, draining vast areas and then waiting for the Depression to pass before developing them. He built a mansion on Key Biscayne, not because he wanted it but because he thought it to be something Bonnie would have enjoyed. He lived there alone with only his household servants.

When World War II came he did his part by serving as chairman of war bond drives and donating money to the USO. Later on, he gave generously to numerous charities and civic projects but never attended social functions, not going out with people.

After the war it started again, another financial boom, not as frenzied as the madness of the 1920s but a boom nevertheless. MacIvey Development surged forward, dredging and filling, building tract houses with their St. Augustine lawns and transplanted cabbage palms, blocking off the ocean beaches with tall buildings, moving westward into the Everglades from Hollywood and Fort Lauderdale and Pompano and Boca Raton and Lake Worth. Sol was no longer an active part of it, turning the management of the company over to young men he hired; but before he realized what was happening he had created something that would not stop until the last swamp was drained, the last tree felled, and the last raccoon left to scrounge scraps from garbage cans or starve.

In 1952 he built his hotel, naming it the La Florida, twenty-five stories of concrete and glass overlooking the ocean on Miami Beach. Again he did it not because he wanted another business but because he remembered the promise he had made that day in Palm Beach so many years ago. When the hotel held its grand opening he did not attend the gala celebration.

More and more he retreated into his private Key Biscayne world, serving as boss of the MacIvey empire in name only, knowing now what was happening but closing his eyes to it, looking the other way. He also withdrew more and more into the past, living in the world of Tobias and Zech, letting his imagination and his memories take him backward in time. The name MacIvey became a phantom, not something real but meaningless letters across bank buildings, art centers and small parks.

Sol sat at the head table, looking out at a sea of faces he did not know and did not want to know. Pounds of diamonds caught the light from glittering chandeliers and magnified it, and women were draped with furs despite the outside heat.

Sol's red hair was now sandy gray, but his lean body was still as ramrod straight as it had ever been. He was dressed in a black suit custom-made by a tailor just for this occasion, patterned after those worn by men before the turn of the century. He also had on a string tie, and looked like a relic taken from a just-opened 1880 time capsule. This was the way he wanted it, and he drew curious glances from everyone in the room, almost all of them seeing him for the first time.

Finally the evening neared the end as a man talked on and on at the microphone. Sol did not listen to the speech, knowing already what would be said about him, but the closing words came through to him, ". . . one of Florida's most important families . . . a man who played a major role in conquering the wilderness and bringing civilization and progress to Florida. . . ."

He got up to thunderous applause and made his way to the podium. He adjusted the mike upward; then he spoke slowly and deliberately, "All that stuff you just heard about me is pure garbage. It's all lies I made up just to see if you would believe it. And it's all a shame on the name of MacIvey. To all those MacIveys who left this earth before me I apologize for telling such whoppers."

He paused for a moment, looking out over an audience now shocked into silence, and then he continued, "My granddaddy wasn't any plantation owner in Georgia. He left there dirt poor and starving, and when he arrived here all he owned was in an ox cart. He didn't start a cattle and citrus empire. He and my granny and my pappa slept on the ground and ate coons and rabbits till he could build a shack to live in. He caught wild cows in the swamps till he had enough to sell the first bunch, and then he went from there.

"I've never been to college one day in my life, much less hold a degree from anywhere. My grampy and granny could not read, and neither could my pappa till he married my mamma and she taught him to read and write. Everything I know she taught me at night beside a coal oil lamp.

"My grampy would never buy the land and never owned so much as a grain of sand. He was a squatter. He believed that no man can own the land, that it all belongs to the Lord, and the Lord lets us stay on awhile as renters. If this is so, and I now believe it's so, then the Lord must be powerful mad at all of us for what we've done to His property. There'll be a day of reckoning for you and for me.

"The first land owned by my pappa was won in a horse race in Punta Rassa, and the first land I bought on Miami Beach was bought with money I earned selling buzzards on the street at Palm Beach.

"It wasn't me who, as was said, 'conquered the wilderness.' I am the least of the MacIveys. It was Tobias MacIvey and Emma and Skillit and Zech and Glenda and Frog and Bonzo and several others I won't even mention. All I did was cash in on what they did. They're buried right now in the middle of an orange grove beside the Kissimmee River, and that's where I'll rest too when the time comes. And it might also interest you to know that my pappa hung enough men to fill this head table. I killed too when I had to.

"The ones who got hurt from all this so-called 'progress' were an old man named Keith Tiger and Tawanda Cypress MacIvey and my half-brother Toby Cypress MacIvey and a bunch more still living out yonder in the swamps in chickees.

"When I first started out alone after my pappa died, I didn't know what I was doing, and I thought I was doing the right thing. But you guys knew, and you did it on purpose. That's the only thing that marks me from you. The catchword with me is stupidity. With you it's greed. More is better, bigger is better. Well, you are too stupid to know there soon won't be no more. Else you haven't been here long enough to remember.

"Too bad for all of you who don't like what I've said here tonight. I don't care about you and you don't care about me, pure and simple. And besides that, you've seen the last of me you'll ever see. I'm going to hide from such as you and pray for forgiveness for what I've helped do. If I could rip out the concrete and put back the woods, I would. But I can't. Progress ain't reversible. What's done is done forever, and I'm sure not proud of it. If any of you idiots had the brains of a jaybird you'd stop right now too. From what we've done to this place in just the past fifty years, what you think it's going to be like in another fifty?"

He stopped abruptly, stepped back and said, "I do thank you kindly for your attention." Then he walked briskly to the nearest exit and left.

♉

Miami, Florida

1968

The silver Rolls Royce glided off Key Biscayne as smoothly as a dolphin cutting the green water of the bay. Solomon MacIvey sat on the back seat, staring at each house they passed, at the spotlessly manicured lawns, as if seeing these things for the first and last time. As they neared the causeway he muttered, "For what this one island is worth today my pappa could have bought the whole state back in 1883 when I was born. Folks has gone as crazy as betsybugs."

"That's right, Mister MacIvey," the driver agreed. "They all gone plumb crazy."

When they came to a park bordered by stately royal palms the old man squinted his tired eyes at the entrance sign: "Solomon MacIvey Park." Then he leaned forward, shook the driver's shoulder and said, "You see that, Arthur. Bought that fifteen acres back in oh-nine for forty-seven dollars and fifty cents. Can you imagine it? And some folks thought I'd been skinned for paying that much. Bet not one soul who uses the park can say who Solomon MacIvey is or could care less. Probably cuss me as some empire-building tycoon who stole everybody blind back in the old days and then gave this park to ease his conscience."

The black driver nodded in agreement as he turned up the avenue. "You sure you want to go through with this, Mister MacIvey?" he asked, knowing what the answer would be but feeling he should ask again for the last time. "I could turn around and go back right now if you'll change your mind."

"I'll not change my mind," MacIvey grunted, "and there'll be no turning back. I don't want to see that big house again. Not ever! Not a single MacIvey died in a fancy place like that, and I won't be the first. We'll go to Punta Rassa as planned, but first I want you to drive up Miami Beach. I want to see it one more time."

"Yes sir, Mister MacIvey. I'll turn across this causeway."

As they crossed the causeway they could see cruise ships making their way into the port, their masts decorated gaily with multi-colored banners. Then the Rolls turned left onto Collins Avenue and moved slowly up South Miami Beach.

The streets here were lined with shabby, rundown apartments and hotels, porches filled with old people sitting in cane-bottom chairs, staring at nothing, some asleep and as yet unnoticed, men and women who had retired from the harsh climate of the North.

"It ain't nothing but a walking cemetery," MacIvey said, staring through heat waves that already drifted up from sidewalks. "Should be turned back to the gulls and terns."

As they continued up Collins Avenue it suddenly changed, as if a boundary line had been drawn across the island, the beach now lined with majestic hotels.

And then they came to the La Florida Hotel, sitting like a stuffed frog, rising above all of them, thirty stories, with the letters MCI across its top. The old man said, "I hope someday it gets blown down. I should 'a never built it in the first place."

From this point north the avenue was lined with motels and cocktail lounges and fast food restaurants and souvenir stores with their display windows stuffed with junk.

MacIvey then said, "That's enough, Arthur. I'd rather try to remember it like it was when I first saw it. Get us off of here at the very next exit."

The driver turned left onto the causeway leading to the mainland.

They turned left again at the mainland, cruising down Biscayne Boulevard, its northern section jammed with more motels and junk food shops, service stations, the sidewalks empty in the early morning sun. Then they came into the downtown business section of Miami, passing the MacIvey State Bank Building with the letters MCI across the front entrance, then Bayfront Park.

The driver slowed and said, "What you want me to do now, Mister MacIvey, head out Highway Forty-one?"

"Not quite yet," he responded. "Before we leave I want to see one more thing. I want you to drive through the area where they had the riot."

"What?" the driver questioned, not sure he had heard right. "How come you want to do that? I've heard it's not all over yet."

"You heard me, Arthur!" the old man snapped. "I want to see! Drive through there!"

"Yes sir, Mister MacIvey," he responded, shaking his head in disagreement but following orders.

He turned left at the next intersection and followed another boulevard, and soon they came to an area of gutted buildings, boarded up storefronts and burned automobiles not yet removed from the streets. People standing idly along sidewalks stared as the car went by.

"They did a pretty good job of it," MacIvey commented as they moved out of the area. "But this isn't the end of it. You mark my words, Arthur, there'll be more, and the next one will be even worse. You bring this many different kinds of people together it's like throwing wolves and panthers into a pen full of cows. The fur never stops flying."

As they moved slowly through the traffic of the lower Tamiami Trail, the old man shook the driver's shoulder again and said, "You know, Arthur, I don't know why some folks was so shocked by the riot. This whole state was born of violence. You can't go anywhere without stepping on the skull of some man or animal that was killed. The whole place is littered with bones."

The driver had heard it all before, but he listened as the old man continued, "What I haven't seen myself I've read about. During these past fourteen years I've holed up in that house alone, I've read enough books to fill up Biscayne Bay. I know about those bloodthirsty Spanish conquistadors who came here with their crosses and killed everything in sight in the name of Christianity. They eventually wiped out all the Indians, the Timucuans, Ais, Calusas, Apalachees, Jeagas, Tekestas. Menendez lopped off the heads of two hundred Frenchmen who came here, and he did it just because they were Huguenots. A British general named Moore took a sweep down here from South Carolina two hundred fifty years ago and killed over six thousand cows and seven thousand Indians. The Seminoles went through it three times, and the third war with them was started because some men in an army survey crew got bored and used ole Billy Bowlegs' pumpkins for target practice. After they shot up his pumpkins, pulled up his beans and squash, and chopped down his banana trees, he complained to them for what they'd done, and there it went again. Another war. And there ain't no telling how many men in my pappa's time was bushwhacked or hung on account of fighting over wild cows. Then later it was over the land itself and the putting up of fences. It went on and on, and it hasn't stopped yet, and most likely never will. You won't find the name of MacIvey in history books, Arthur, but they were right in the thick of it. And I mean the thick! We scattered a few bones too."

"Yes sir, Mister MacIvey. I know what you say is the truth."

By now they had left the city and entered the Everglades with its endless stretches of open sawgrass dotted with distant hammocks of hardwood and palm. The road and both shoulders were littered with the decaying bodies of small animals struck by automobiles. Buzzards flapped out of the way as the car approached, and then returned as soon as it passed.

Soon they came to the Miccosukee Indian Reservation bordering the highway, an area lined with airboat rides and tourist villages and craft stores, and after this they entered the Big Cypress Swamp.

The old man studied the passing landscape carefully. "Slow down, Arthur, so I can get my bearings," he cautioned. "It's been a while since I've been here." After another three miles he said, "Turn right at the next dirt trail."

The tires on the car made crunching sounds as it glided slowly along a sandy road heavily lined with palmetto and pond cypress. A mother raccoon with her brood of babies scurried out of the way as they made a sharp turn and came into the edge of a clearing. MacIvey said, "Stop here and wait. It could be we'll have another passenger."

Several chickee huts were spaced around the clearing, and beneath one of them an old woman stirred a cooking pot with a wooden spoon. MacIvey approached her and said, "I'm looking for Toby Cypress."

Without speaking she pointed toward a chickee at the far side of the clearing.

MacIvey hesitated for a moment, looking around the Seminole village, remembering the first time he had come here over seventy years ago, seeing that nothing had changed except faces. Then he walked to the chickee and found an old man sitting beside it, his hair solid white, his sun-baked skin as wrinkled as cypress bark. He seemed to be asleep as MacIvey said, "Toby Cypress?"

The old Indian squinted and said, "Yes. I am Toby Cypress. What is it you wish of me?"

"Don't you know who I am?"

Toby Cypress pushed himself up and looked closer, and then he smiled. "Sol MacIvey! It has been many decades now, and age has changed both of us, but I would still know you. It is only a MacIvey who is so tall and lanky. Sit here with me and tell me why you have come back to the village after all this time."

178

MacIvey settled himself to the ground in front of Toby Cypress and said, "You haven't changed so much, Toby. Do you still ride a marshtackie like the wind?"

"No, Sol. I have not been on a horse for so long now I don't remember. All I do is sit in the chickee like an old woman. I am growing tired of it."

"We sure used to ride, didn't we?" MacIvey said, remembering fondly. "And we had some good times together too. I've thought of them often. And I've kept track of you through the years although I haven't been back here. I know you served for a long time as tribal leader and did many good things for your people."

"Yes, this is so. We now have two reservations, but I've never lived there. I would rather stay here in the swamp where I belong. But many of my people live there, and we have cattle once again. But tell me, why have you come back now like a ghost from the past?"

"I'm on my way to Punta Rassa, to live my last days at the cabin Pappa built there. I've left my house in Miami and will never return to it. I would rather see things as they once were."

"There is no more Punta Rassa as you knew it," Toby Cypress said, his eyes reflecting sadness. "It is all gone, Sol, just as Lake Okeechobee as we once knew it is gone, and the custard-apple forest is gone, and the bald cypress trees are gone. You are trying to capture the fog, and no one can do that."

"The cabin is still there, as good as ever, and the land too. I came to ask you to go with me. We can hunt and fish, and plant a garden, and be close like we once were."

Toby Cypress picked up a stick and scratched in the dirt, and then he said, "There is a Seminole legend that says when an old man knows he is going to die, he goes off alone into the woods, searching for the place of his birth. That is what you are doing now, Sol. I will make the same journey very soon. But we must each do it in our own way. I cannot go with you to Punta Rassa."

"I suppose not, Toby, but I just thought I'd ask. But I do want to part with you this last time as friends and as a brother, like it used to be. I'm sorry we broke away in anger those many years ago."

"I am sorry too, and I am no longer angry at you for destroying the land as you did. But, Sol, it could have never been different with us. We are brothers only because we had the same father. My mother was Seminole, and yours white, and we were born to live in different worlds. There was no other way. We have each lived our lives as we had to, and now we depart in different ways. But know this, Sol. I have always loved our father, Zech MacIvey, just as my mother loved him. And I have loved you too. I have no hatred in my heart. Believe this now, and we will go in peace."

"That's what I wanted to hear," MacIvey said, his face relieved. "I have no children, Toby, and I am the last of the MacIveys. It ends with me, and that is my biggest regret from the way I messed up my life. But the MacIvey blood runs on in the veins of your sons, and I want you to know I'm proud of this. Pappa would be proud too. And there's another thing I want you to know. All the land I still own that hasn't been turned into concrete, and there is a great deal of it, including the land south of Okeechobee and along the Kissimmee River, I am turning into a preserve where the animals can live again as they once did."

"That is good," Toby Cypress replied, pleased, "but do it soon before there are no more birds in the sky and no more creatures on the land."

"It's already done. And all the money I leave behind will be spent to buy more land for preserves. It's the least I can do now to make up for the bad things I've done in the past. Things I'm not proud of, Toby. And there's a great deal of money to do this, more than you can imagine." He then got up and said, "It's time for me to go now, Toby. We won't see each other again, so I'll say farewell—and happy hunting."

Toby Cypress pushed himself up slowly, then he grasped

MacIvey's hand. "Goodbye, Sol. Brother. We are both part of a time that is no more, and it is good that it ends soon for both of us. I hope you capture the fog and find a small part of it again in your last days."

The two old men stood facing each other, Solomon MacIvey gripping the wrinkled brown hands tightly; then he turned and walked away. He did not look back as the car retraced its way down the sandy trail.

✝

CHAPTER FORTY-FIVE

Punta Rassa

1968

Just before noon they came to the southern outskirts of Naples and into a logjam of traffic, cars and trucks moving slowly bumper to bumper, impatient drivers blaring horns and shaking fists at each other in anger. Both sides of the highway were lined solidly with fast food joints and service stations and shopping centers. When they stopped for a traffic light the driver said, "You want to stop now and get something to eat, Mister MacIvey? And it's time for your pill."

MacIvey snapped. "We'll wait till we get there to eat. All we'd do here is choke to death on carbon monoxide."

The trip became slower and slower until finally they turned from the main highway and followed a two-lane road leading toward the Gulf. It skirted the south bank of the Caloosahatchie River and then turned back inland.

Once again the car glided down a sandy road lined with palmetto, and presently they came to a locked gate. After opening the gate the driver moved the car into a one-hundred-fifty-acre jungle of cabbage palms and hickory and oaks surrounded by a fence topped with three strands of barbed wire.

The cabin, located in the center of the forest, was made of cypress boards weathered black but still sturdy and well preserved. The open area around it was freshly mowed. At the edge of the clearing, directly behind the cabin, there was an outhouse and a storage shed.

MacIvey got out of the car and said, "This cabin is older than I am, Arthur, but it's still as good as it was when Pappa built it. They don't make lumber like that no more. And this is one piece of land that'll never feel the bite of a bulldozer blade. I've seen to that."

As soon as everything had been carried inside, MacIvey said, "Fetch us a couple of cans of beans and some coffee, Arthur. We'll eat at the table out here."

The driver hesitated, and then he said, "You know you not supposed to drink coffee, Mister MacIvey. And you still haven't taken a pill. I put your pill bottle on the stand beside the bed."

"You can just take it back to Miami with you!" the old man said. "I'm not taking any more pills! And I'm not having some crabby nurse hovering over me all the time, telling me what I can eat and drink and what I can't! Why do you think I came up here?"

The driver said gently, trying to calm the old man, "I'm just trying to help, Mister MacIvey. You done had two heart attacks, and you know what the doctor said about the pills."

"I know what he said, and I don't want to hear another word about it! Now you go on and fetch us something to eat like I said!"

"Yes sir, Mister MacIvey."

The two of them sat at a cypress table facing each other, eating from the cans with spoons. MacIvey took a huge bite, washed it down with strong coffee and said, "That's good, Arthur. Nothing's more fittin' for a man than beans, but the doctor says I can't eat them no more. Causes too much gas. I'll have 'em again for breakfast in the morning. I've eaten enough beans to bury that doctor and I'm still here. I'll bet I'm the only eighty-five-year-old cracker left with all his own teeth. Wasn't for this bad heart I could go another eighty-five years. But I wouldn't want to, not the way things are now. I've seen too much as it is. My pappa and my grampy would have strokes if they could see what's happened since they left. That road we came over today, Arthur, with the fancy name of Tamiami Trail. Before it was finished back in twenty-eight, it took ten days to cross the Everglades to Miami, and we made the same trip this morning in three hours. But my pappa wouldn't want to see it. He'd rather go by horse and canoe and take the ten days. He'd say, 'What's the awful hurry?'" He suddenly changed the subject. "How long you been working for me, Arthur?"

The black man scratched his gray head and tried to think, counting on his fingers. He finally said, "'Bout thirty years, Mister MacIvey. Ever since I wandered into your place broker than a haint and you gave me a job tendin' the yard."

"You like to drive that Rolls, don't you?"

"Yessir, I sure do. It beats those clunkers we had back during the war. But they was all we could get then."

"Well, that one is yours now. I've already had the title changed. You can do whatever you want with it."

Surprise flashed into Arthur's face, and then pleasure. "I rightly thank you, Mister MacIvey! I never thought I'd own a car like that. But you didn't have to do it."

"I know I didn't have to!" MacIvey shot back. "A man my age don't have to do anything, including worrying about what he puts in his belly. I did it because I want to. I've also set up a trust fund in your name that will give you all the money you need for the rest of your life. The lawyer will tell you about it when you get back to Miami. You can take off that chauffeur suit whenever you want to and throw it right into the middle of Biscayne Bay."

"Thank you, Mister MacIvey!" Arthur exclaimed, his voice trembling. Then he reached over and grabbed the old man's hand.

"I was worried sick about what I'd do when you left! I don't know what to say, Mister MacIvey!"

"Then don't say nothing. And don't get carried away and slobber on me. I can't stand to see a man slobber. And it's about time you headed back to Miami."

They got up and walked to the car together. MacIvey said, "You can come back in a week and bring more grub. The grounds keeper is out here every morning checking on things, so don't worry about me. And don't tell a soul where I am. You understand?"

"Yes sir, I understand. I won't tell a soul." He suddenly grabbed MacIvey, hugged the frail body tightly and said, "I thanks you again, Mister MacIvey! God bless you!"

"Arthur!" the old man roared. "I done told you not to slobber on me! Now git!"

He watched briefly as the car turned around and headed back along the sandy lane, then he muttered, "Folks nowadays think a old man can't take care of himself and make it alone. I never knew a MacIvey to need a nursemaid, and I don't either. I'll throw them pills out for the buzzards to eat."

Then he went inside the cabin and slammed the door.

*M*orning sunlight streamed through the east window as Sol sat in a cane-bottom rocker, staring at an old board tacked to the wall. Its white letters were badly faded but still readable: MACIVEY CATTLE COMPANY. Sunbeams seemed to catch in the ancient paint and make it glitter. The glow hurt his eyes, so he got up and closed the curtains.

Just beside the window there was a gun rack containing several Winchesters and a ten-gauge double-barreled shotgun. He picked up the shotgun and aimed it, its tremendous weight pulling his frail arms downward. He cocked one hammer and squeezed the trigger, hearing a sharp click as the firing pin popped into an empty chamber; then he put it back into the rack beside a rusty branding iron.

He crossed the room and took one of the two whips from a dresser drawer; then he went outside and popped it. The awesome sound sent a frightened rabbit bounding away. He cracked it again and again, seeing ghostly cows scatter in front of him, and then he felt a hot pain sear through his chest.

There was a cypress bench beside the cabin porch, and he staggered to it and sat down. Sweat poured from his face as he remembered himself racing across the clearing on Tiger and jumping the split-rail fence, going after Zech as he rode south seeking the outlaws. He heard his mother shout, "Sol MacIvey! You come back here this instant!"

For a moment he thought of going inside and searching for the pill bottle, but Bonnie seemed to come and sit beside him, and he forgot the pills.

Then suddenly they were all out there looking at him, MacIveys all, burned brown by prairie sun and wind, living and loving and dying, one by one bidding him farewell as they faded back into the harsh glow of sunlight, leaving him alone again.

The pain increased as his tired eyes squinted and looked after them, seeing them come and go now, Zech galloping wildly on a marshtackie, Skillit throwing a bull with just a twist of his powerful body, Frog stuffing himself with stew as Emma put more bowls on the table, Glenda in her jeans and boots, Bonnie's ponytail flapping as wind rushed through the open Model T. As his eyes glazed, the last one to appear was Tobias, looking like a living scarecrow in his faded overalls and wide-brimmed hat, leading all of them, heading westward toward Punta Rassa.

He gazed to the west where the shipping port had once been, straining to hear the bellowing of penned cows, hearing instead the roar of gasoline engines somewhere to the north. He said weakly, "Where did it all go, Pappa?. . . Where did it all go?. . ."

The last sound he heard as the whip dropped from his hand was a dove calling mournfully for a missing mate.

If you enjoyed reading this book, here are some other books from Pineapple Press for young people. For a complete catalog, write to Pineapple Press, P.O. Box 3899, Sarasota, FL 34230 or call 1-800-PINEAPL (746-3275). Or visit our website at www.pineapplepress.com.

The Florida Water Story by Peggy Sias Lantz and Wendy A. Hale. Illustrates and describes many of the plants and animals that depend on the springs, rivers, beaches, marshes, and reefs in and around Florida. ISBN 1-56164-099-9 (hb)

The Young Naturalist's Guide to Florida by Peggy Sias Lantz and Wendy A. Hale. Complete with a glossary, this enticing book shows young readers where and how to look for Florida's most interesting natural features and creatures. ISBN 1-56164-051-4 (pb)

Native Americans in Florida by Kevin M. McCarthy. Teaches about the many diverse Indian tribes in Florida from prehistoric times to the present. Also includes information about archaeology, an extensive glossary, and legends that teach moral lessons. ISBN 1-56164-181-2 (hb); ISBN 1-56164-182-0 (pb); ISBN 1-56164-188-X (teacher's manual)

African Americans in Florida by Maxine D. Jones and Kevin M. McCarthy. Profiles African Americans during four centuries of Florida history in brief essays. ISBN 1-56164-030-1 (hb); ISBN 1-56164-031-X (pb); ISBN 1-56164-045-X (teacher's manual)

The Spy Who Came In from the Sea by Peggy Nolan. Teenager Frank Hollahan moves to Florida in 1943 at the height of World War II. He soon becomes entangled in a mystery involving a German spy that ends up teaching him valuable lessons about friendship, perseverance, and the power of the truth. ISBN 1-56164-186-3 (hb)

Legends of the Seminoles by Betty Mae Jumper. Illustrated in color, this book contains Seminole legends that have never existed in print before. For readers and listeners of all ages. ISBN 1-56164-033-6 (hb); ISBN 1-56164-040-9 (pb)

CRACKER WESTERNS:

A series of adventure-packed cowboy stories set right here in Florida. Historically accurate and fun to read.

Ghosts of the Green Swamp by Lee Gramling. Saddle up your easy chair and kick back for a Cracker Western featuring that rough-and-ready but soft-hearted Florida cowboy, Tate Barkley, introduced in *Riders of the Suwannee*. ISBN 1-56164-120-0 (hb); 1-56164-126-X (pb)

Guns of the Palmetto Plains by Rick Tonyan. As the Civil War explodes over Florida, Tree Hooker dodges Union soldiers and Florida outlaws to drive cattle to feed the starving Confederacy. ISBN 1-56164-061-1 (hb); 1-56164-070-0 (pb)

Riders of the Suwannee by Lee Gramling. Tate Barkley returns to 1870s' Florida just in time to come to the aid of a young widow and her children as they fight to save their homestead from outlaws. ISBN 1-56164-046-8 (hb); 1-56164-043-3 (pb)

Thunder on the St. Johns by Lee Gramling. Riverboat gambler Chance Ramsay teams up with the family of young Josh Carpenter and the trapper's daughter Abby Macklin to combat a slew of greedy outlaws seeking to destroy the dreams of honest homesteaders. ISBN 1-56164-064-6 (hb); 1-56164-080-8 (pb)

Trail from St. Augustine by Lee Gramling. A young trapper, a crusty ex-sailor, and an indentured servant girl fleeing a cruel master join forces to cross the Florida wilderness in search of buried treasure and a new life. ISBN 1-56164-047-6 (hb); 1-56164-042-5 (pb)